Amanda ... **registere...**

"The livesto...

"*Ya.*"

"You're going to show them?"

"*Ya.*"

"Oh." Amanda felt her guard go back up. David Troyer was competition.

He watched her reaction. "What? Is there a problem with the show?"

"*Ya.* There is."

He frowned. "What is it?"

"I'm entering it too."

David raised his eyebrows, then let out a long, low whistle. "*Vell*, may the best man—or woman—win."

"You stole my line."

He tipped his straw hat, grinned at her and sauntered past. He scooped up the package of vitamins as he walked by it. "*Danki* for the tip," David said without looking back.

Amanda clenched her fists. She watched him casually stroll to the counter, set the package down and make small talk with someone. He was cutting into her territory, her world. He did not belong here. And now he was the one gloating—after *she* had apologized!

Now she really had to win that livestock competition. She would show him what she was made of, that was certain sure.

Virginia Wise combines her love of romance, family and Plain living to create uplifting stories set in idyllic Amish communities. Her favorite pastimes include wandering Lancaster County's Amish country and meeting new people who inspire her novels. She also loves meeting the people who read her books and is always eager to hear from them. When she's not working, Virginia enjoys painting, spending time with family and friends, and taking long walks in the woods.

Books by Virginia Wise

Love Inspired

An Amish Christmas Inheritance
The Secret Amish Admirer
Healed by the Amish Nanny
A Home for His Amish Children
The Amish Baby Scandal

Sisters of Stoneybrook Farm

His Amish Christmas Surprise
Falling for the Amish Rival

Visit the Author Profile page at LoveInspired.com.

FALLING FOR THE AMISH RIVAL

VIRGINIA WISE

LOVE INSPIRED
INSPIRATIONAL ROMANCE

LOVE INSPIRED®
INSPIRATIONAL ROMANCE

ISBN-13: 978-1-335-62137-5

Falling for the Amish Rival

Copyright © 2026 by Virginia Wise

Love Inspired
22 Adelaide St. West, 41st Floor
Toronto, Ontario M5H 4E3, Canada
www.LoveInspired.com

HarperCollins Publishers
Macken House, 39/40 Mayor Street Upper,
Dublin 1, D01 C9W8, Ireland
www.HarperCollins.com

Printed in Lithuania

Recycling programs for this product may not exist in your area.

Now there are diversities of gifts, but the same Spirit.
—*1 Corinthians* 12:4

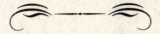

To Maria and Laura

Chapter One

Dear L.D.,

I need to be outside, where I can spread my arms wide and race through the pastureland. There's just something about being beneath an open sky that makes me feel free. That doesn't sound silly to you, does it? I get the feeling you understand. I know you love your farm as much as I love mine.

It's funny that two pen pals who've never met could have so much in common. I'm pretty sure you're the only person who gets why I love farming more than housework. Sure, I know how to cook, clean, sew and all that. But after my father died, my brother was the only one left on our goat farm to do the men's work, so I've been able to get away with doing those chores, since he needed help. My sisters have to do a good bit of the farmwork too. It takes a team effort to keep this place running. But they don't love it like I do.

Write back soon and let me know how your goats are doing. I hope the advice I gave you in my last letter helped.

Sincerely,

M.M.

David Troyer's stomach churned as he strode into the enormous sheet-metal barn where the auction was being held. Everything counted on him right now. He could not afford to make a single mistake. He had sunk all the money he had into his new goat farm. If it failed, he would have to go back to work at the factory, building modular homes. Good thing he had a pen pal to give him much-needed advice. He and M.M. had never met, but she had been writing for months, walking him through the steps he needed to take—and sharing a bit about herself. The more he learned about her, the more he admired her. It was hard to keep their relationship strictly business, even if it was just on paper. He had to remind himself that M.M. had no idea who he really was, so nothing could ever come of the relationship, even if he wanted it to. She didn't even know his full name. He signed his letters using the initials *L.D.*, because most folks called him Lloyd's David. There were too many Davids in his family, so the Amish used his father's name, Lloyd, to identify which David he was.

The familiar, earthy smells of hay and farm animals met David as he walked through Byler Brothers' Livestock Market. The space was filled with the low murmur of voices, the clattering of metal, the lowing of cattle and the soft whinny of horses. These were the sounds and scents that David loved, that he remembered from childhood—before things got too tough and his father had to sell up and move the family to a little apartment in town. David would have worked on his family's farm as soon as he left school after the eighth grade, but instead he'd had to take odd jobs for Amish families until he was old enough to work for the *Englisch*. Then he'd gotten a job at the factory alongside his father and the other Amish men in his church district who didn't own farms or small businesses.

David's father had not minded building modular homes for a living. He said it was good, honest work and the repetitive nature felt soothing and gave him plenty of time to think. But David had hated it. He'd longed for the independence of the farm, where there was no boss looking over his shoulder, where he didn't have to clock in or clock out, where he had control over his own schedule. Most of all he had missed being outdoors, living in the natural rhythm of the seasons, each day different depending on the weather.

David found the sales office in the front corner of the barn and registered for a bidder number. After filling out the registration card and grabbing a sales catalog, he wound through the crowd to the ring. The big, open space crackled with energy as people climbed onto the bleachers and the livestock moved restlessly in their pens. David studied the sales catalog as more people spilled onto the bleachers and the noise level grew. There were *Englisch* farmers in jeans and baseball caps and Amish men dressed just like him in solid-colored shirts with suspenders, black broadfall trousers and straw hats.

David jumped a little when the auctioneer's voice boomed over the loudspeaker. He straightened up on the metal bleacher and focused. He wanted to be sure to get this right. There was only one group of Angoras for auction and he needed to win the bid. He might not get another chance like this for a long time. He was hoping to invest the last of his savings into a few more goats to up his fiber production. It was a risk, but he believed it would be worth it. It was all or nothing at this point. He only had a few more weeks to increase his earnings before the entire operation would go belly-up and he would have to return to his old life, his dream lost forever.

David looked back over the sales catalog and shuffled his feet while the sheep came through, followed by some rabbits, until finally the goats came into the ring. His hand was the first to shoot up when the auctioneer opened the bidding.

A few other hands waved in the air each time the auctioneer droned out the prices in his funny, too-fast way of speaking. David had to concentrate to keep up. It was all moving so quickly. After a few more bids, the hands stopped waving, until David was the only one. He grinned and waited for the auctioneer to slam down his gavel and shout "Sold!" But instead, he upped the price again and asked in his rapid speech, "Do-we-have-another-bidder-another-bidder-at-this-price-yes-we-do! Two-bidders-left."

David jerked around to peer behind him, his hand still in the air. A small Amish woman in an emerald-green cape dress was waving at the auctioneer. She had a look of fierce determination on her face.

David frowned and turned back around. He could not let her outbid him. He needed these goats. She raised the bid again. Then one more time. And another. David turned around again and caught the woman's eye. She raised an eyebrow and gave a sly smile, as if she already knew that she would win. David felt a jolt of irritation as he turned back to face the ring. He was annoyed because he knew that she was right. She was going to win. He just wished that she could be a little more gracious about it.

"Any other bidders?" the auctioneer called out. David's chest tightened. Should he go higher? Could he afford the investment? No. He could not. His heart sank as he forced himself to keep his hand down. Everything in him shouted to raise it just one more time to try to win. "Going-once-going-twice-and-sold-to-the-young-lady-in-the-green-dress." Bang went the gavel.

And then it was over. Just like that. David had lost the bid and would go home empty-handed. He knew he wouldn't get another opportunity to buy top Angoras at an affordable price. Or what should have been an affordable price if that woman hadn't been there to drive it up.

He glanced back at her and tried not to notice how cute she looked as she flashed a victory smile at him. Her dark eyes gleamed, and her tanned face was flushed with excitement. A strand of dark brown hair had slipped out of her *kapp*, which made him want to gently tuck it back behind her ear. Stop. He would not think the enemy was cute. Okay, maybe she wasn't an enemy exactly, but she sure felt like it right now. She was a rival, at the very least.

"May the best man—or woman—win, ain't so?" she said as she pushed the loose hair beneath her *kapp*. Her smile widened and David thought it had a distinctly smug look to it.

He grunted and turned back around so that he didn't have to respond. He should have offered a friendly "Congratulations," but he couldn't force himself to say the words. This was probably just fun and games for her. Her farm wasn't on the line right now. But his sure was. And now he would have to keep it going with the goats that he already had, before time ran out. *Please, Gott, help me to succeed*, he thought as he stood up, then picked his way down the bleachers. Two elderly *Englischer* men in overalls cut in front of him and slowed his pace. He tapped his fingers against his leg as he made little half steps. He could hear the woman in the green dress laughing and chatting behind him.

"I knew I'd get that lot," she said to someone else. "I always have a plan."

"This time it was close," a woman replied.

"*Nee*," the woman in green said. "It just looked that way. I knew exactly what I was doing."

The other woman laughed. "You sound pretty prideful, *ya*?"

"Prideful?" The woman paused. "I just knew what to do, that's all."

David had thought she sounded prideful too, but she seemed confused when she replied to her companion, as if pride were the last thing on her mind. David wanted to look back at her, but resisted. He wondered what her story was. He wished he wasn't interested, but he remembered the flash in her eyes and the excited flush in her cheeks and felt an annoying curiosity. He had never seen an Amish woman take that kind of initiative at an auction. It made him admire her. A little bit, anyway. He was still irritated. But also intrigued.

Not that it mattered. He would never see her again.

He was wrong. After he stopped for a soft pretzel at the auction food stand, he wandered past the goat pen on the way out. And there she was, leaning against the fence with her palms resting on the top. She looked casual and confident, and her eyes were still gleaming as she gazed down at the goats that she had scooped out from under him. "Just look how cute they all are!" she gushed to the woman beside her. "I want to hug each and every one of them."

"I'm sure you will," her companion said. She was small and had dark features like the woman in green, but her build was stouter and her expression more serious. David suspected that they were sisters, due to their resemblance.

"Miriam, stop using that tone with me. How can you not love these little guys as much as I do?"

"I don't love them or hate them," Miriam said. "They're goats. They serve their purpose, that's all."

The woman in green sighed. "*Ach*, how can you be so cynical? They are the cutest little things you've ever seen, and you know it!"

"I'm not cynical, I'm practical. Now let's get the paperwork signed and get going. There's dinner to get on the table. I've got to start on the bread so it has time to rise."

"Okay, fine." But instead of leaving, the woman in green stepped up onto the bottom fence slat so that she could get closer to the goats. She shimmied up the fence, until she was leaning into the pen from the waist up, her feet dangling off the ground.

"Amanda!" Miriam said. "Watch it. You're going to fall in."

So, Amanda was her name.

"I'm not going to fall in!" Amanda hissed, then scooted a little farther over the top of the fence. "I just want to pet that cute little goat, right there. I need to get a little closer."

David shook his head. Amanda only wanted a pet. He

had been right about her. She wasn't a serious farmer. She probably wasn't a farmer at all, just an animal lover who thought she should get whatever she wanted. She had outbid him just so that she could cuddle the "cute little goats," not to make a living. He sighed and started to turn away.

"Amanda, watch it," Miriam said.

"Just a little closer—"

David caught a flash of movement out of the corner of his eye. Amanda was sliding into the pen, headfirst. He cut the distance between them in one quick step, lunged forward and grabbed her by the waist. She gasped as his arms caught her. He tried not to think about how close she was to him as he held her tightly, then hauled her up and over the fence. She was fine boned and short, so she hardly weighed anything at all. He gently set her onto her feet, dropped his arms and stepped away from her.

She looked stunned for a few beats, then her eyes moved upward and she tilted her head back to peer up at him. Their eyes met and David felt himself sinking into them. They were dark, full of depth and passion. He cleared his throat. His thoughts were going to strange places. He had to reel them in. He reminded himself that she was a careless person who had just done a careless thing and almost gotten hurt. Plus, she had beaten him out of a good bunch of Angoras. So why was she having such an effect on him? "You okay?" he asked in a brisk, distant tone. "That was a close call."

"Um, *ya*. I'm okay." She stared up at him in a way that made his heart flutter. "*Danki*."

David shifted his weight from one foot to the other and looked away. He was confused about how to feel. He had been so annoyed with Amanda a moment ago… No, there was nothing to be confused about. He just needed to remember the facts and walk away. "You should be more careful," he said in a tone that came out harsher than he meant.

Amanda's expression dropped, then hardened. "I can take care of myself."

"Doesn't look like it. You would have gone face-first into the goat pen if I hadn't been here."

"I was just about to catch myself."

"Right. Sure, you were."

"I was!" She crossed her arms. "Anyway, we'll never know now."

"Because I interrupted your fall?"

"Ya."

"So, I should have let you keep falling and land on your head?"

"I just told you that I wasn't going to fall on my head."

"Uh-huh. *Oll recht.* You were going head-first intentionally. Got it. Just remember that the next time you want to cuddle your cute little pets, I won't be here to help you."

"Cute little pets?" Amanda snorted. "You're just annoyed that I outbid you. That's why you're being so combative."

"I saved you. That's the opposite of combative."

"Saved me? Humph." Amanda lifted her chin a fraction higher.

"Ya. And now I'm leaving. Some of us have actual farms to run."

"Actual farms to run?" Amanda glared at him. "I cannot believe you just said that."

"*Vell*, it's only the truth."

"You don't know the first thing about me or my farm."

"I know enough." David turned and strode away before he allowed the conversation to go any further. For a moment, when she had stared up at him with those big, thoughtful eyes, he had felt a spark for this woman who was clearly a very bad match for him. Thankfully, he had let common sense prevail. He let out a deep breath. That could have been a disaster. Good thing they were unlikely to ever run into each other again. Because David knew he had to stay far away from Amanda. Otherwise, he might fall for a rival who could never understand him or the challenges he faced. And that would end up hurting everyone involved.

Amanda was furious. How dare that man say that she was not a serious farmer? He had no idea of the hours and hours she put into her work every day. And all the nights that she stayed awake, straining to read by lantern light to learn more about raising goats. He thought she just kept them as a hobby. "Cute little pets," he had said. Just because she loved her goats and thought each one was adorable didn't mean that they were pets. The man at the auction had treated her like most of the men she knew did—or the ones who had tried to court her, anyway. The last time a suitor drove her home from a singing, he had asked, "Don't you like anything besides goat farming? You know, normal stuff, like cooking or baking or quilting?"

Normal stuff? Ha! Goat farming was what she loved, and she would not pretend to be anyone else but who she was, even if that meant being single for the rest of her life.

Which it probably would.

She wished that Amish buggies had doors that slammed like *Englisch* cars so that she could make a dramatic exit when she and her siblings got back to Stoneybrook Farm. Instead, she had to slink away quietly, fists clenched at her sides.

"Are you still mad?" her brother, Benjamin, asked as he began to unhitch Clyde, their buggy horse. "I saw the whole thing, you know. You could have said thank you when that man caught you."

Amanda did not respond. Instead, she marched past her sisters, Miriam and Naomi, as they climbed down from the buggy. She stalked across the farmyard and pounded up the worn front porch steps of the big, weathered farmhouse, tore open the screen door and let it bang behind her as she raced up a steep flight of stairs to her bedroom.

The room was plain but cozy with a four-poster bed, a row of colorful cape dresses hanging from pegs on the wall and a small wooden desk with a kerosene lantern on top. Alongside the lamp lay a disordered stack of books, mostly about goats and fiber production. Amanda locked the door behind her, then strode to the window and jerked down the green shade, dimming the space and muffling the sound of bleating goats in the distance. She knew it was overkill to cover the window, but with four nosy siblings roaming the property, one could never be too careful. She ran the farm along with her sisters, Miriam, Naomi and Leah, and their brother, Benjamin. Leah's new husband, John, and his baby, Abby, along with Benjamin's wife, Emma, and her baby, Benjamin—who they had nicknamed Caleb to prevent confusion—lived with them too. It was a very full house, which was another reason that Amanda liked being outdoors with the goats. It gave her privacy and space to think.

Amanda hurried to the bed, dropped to her knees, pushed aside the colorful nine-patch quilt and patted the bare floorboards until her fingers hit a small, wooden chest. She sighed as she pulled it out from beneath the bed, then gently flipped the latch and opened the lid. A stack of envelopes lay inside, neatly organized by date received. Each one bore the same PO box return address. Each one had the same loose cursive on familiar yellow notepaper. Each one was a reminder that someone, somewhere appreciated her, even though they had never met. Amanda picked a letter from the top of the stack, pressed it against her chest and breathed in deeply. She had not meant to let her emotions get the best of her. She had not meant to develop feelings for a stranger who would never be more than a pen pal. This relationship was supposed to be strictly business. And for the man on the other side of that PO box, it surely was.

So, what was the matter with her? What kind of Amish woman developed a secret crush on a man she didn't even know? And what kind of Amish woman preferred tending goats and doing heavy farmwork over housework? According to the boys who had courted her, she wasn't supposed to feel this way. That was what they had all told her.

None of them had courted her for very long. Not after they got to know her. She was too different, they said. She didn't want the same things they wanted, they explained. As far as Amanda could tell, what they wanted was for someone to cook and clean for them, to wash their clothes and keep their house and never complain about any of it. Well, she enjoyed being outside, not shut up indoors baking, scrubbing and dusting. Did that make her unfit for marriage?

Apparently, it did.

But L.D. didn't think so. Well, he had never called her *marriageable* exactly—they never talked about anything as personal as that—but he appreciated her insight on animal husbandry and farming techniques. He asked for her advice and took it, without being insecure about it. He didn't feel threatened by her competence. He shared his insights with her too, but was quick to admit that he was new to raising goats and didn't know as much as she did. They wrote about their trials and triumphs, funny anecdotes about their goats, and encouraged each other to keep up the good work. It was a wonderful friendship.

So wonderful that Amanda longed for it to be more than friendship. But she could never tell L.D. that. She didn't even know his full name, only the initials he used to sign his letters. She didn't know what he looked like either, but she could imagine. In fact, she spent far too much time doing so.

They had begun corresponding after L.D. saw a flyer that Amanda had posted on a bulletin board at a farm supply store. She'd been advertising some used milking tables that she wanted to sell after her family had upgraded to new ones. Amanda had not put her name on the advertisement because she was afraid that other farmers might not take her seriously if they knew she was a young woman. She'd used the initials *M.M.*, for

Mini Manda, Benjamin's nickname for her. And she'd used the PO box that they used for all their business correspondence, so L.D. didn't know to whom he was writing when he responded to the notice. As it turned out, he didn't want to buy the tables, but he did want advice, and figured she must know something about milking goats. They had hit it off right away. On paper, anyway. Amanda loved talking about goats and rarely found anyone who wanted to listen. For some strange reason, most people found the topic boring after the first twenty minutes or so. But not L.D.

He didn't know that she co-owned Stoneybrook Farm, only that she ran a prosperous goat farm somewhere in Lancaster County. She wondered if he had guessed, since Stoneybrook Farm was the biggest goat farm in the area. But he lived in a different church district—one that didn't interact with hers, because it was a long buggy ride away—so maybe he had not put it together. Because they were Amish, there weren't any photos of her on the internet. There was no way for him to look up images of the women who owned goat farms in Lancaster County, if he bent the rules and went online.

Amanda slapped the letter back into the chest and slammed the lid. L.D. could be ninety-five years old for all she knew. He could be an ex-felon. He could be anything. But her heart said that he was someone special. Hearts were silly, fickle things, though. That was what her big sister Miriam liked to say, anyway. Miriam had managed to raise Amanda, Leah, Naomi and Benjamin after their parents died in an automobile accident twelve years ago, with a hired *Englisch* driver at the wheel. After taking on their parents' role, Miriam never listened to her heart. She was tough as nails, still single and never once complained about it. Amanda wanted to be the same way. But she couldn't help longing for someone who understood her and appreciated her for who she was. And she had found that man in L.D., whoever he was.

She knew very little about him. Each letter focused more on farming than on their personal lives. But of course, that *was* her personal life. What about his personal life, though? "I don't even know him," Amanda muttered as she shoved the chest back under the bed. All she knew was that he was Amish, shared her love of farming and was unmarried. Nearly everything else about his personal life was a mystery. A mystery that she kept from her family. They wouldn't understand a secret correspondence. She wasn't sure she even understood herself.

Amanda stood up and smoothed her apron. Enough nonsense. She needed to focus on what mattered, not foolish thoughts about a man she had never met. It was time to take care of the evening milking.

When she sat down at the table for supper, Amanda's thoughts turned back to the man at the auction. Benjamin had to ask her twice to pass the green beans, and Naomi had to nudge her to make her stop drumming her fingers on the big oak table. They were eating in the spacious dining room, with its creaky wooden floors, tall farmhouse windows, sideboard filled with an extra set of mismatched dishes and hand-sewn place mats on the table that looked like little patchwork quilts.

"She only does that when she's mad," Miriam said before taking a bite of sweet-potato casserole.

"I'm not mad," Amanda said.

Miriam set down her fork. "Sure you are. You've been out of sorts ever since that man had to save you from falling into the goat pen."

"That's not what happened."

Miriam raised an eyebrow.

"*Vell*, not exactly," Amanda said and looked down.

"Wait, you fell into the goat pen?" Emma asked. She had stayed home with baby Caleb and now she was holding him at the dinner table, rocking him slowly while eating with her free hand.

"*Nee*. I already said that's not what happened."

"Because a handsome stranger swooped in and rescued her," Miriam said.

"Stop making fun of me," Amanda said as she speared a slab of pot roast with her fork.

"So, he wasn't *gut*-looking?" Miriam deadpanned.

Amanda scowled at her plate. "That is completely irrelevant." The truth was that he had been good-looking. His bright blue eyes, tousled brown hair and spray of freckles had caught her attention as soon as she laid eyes on him. And then, when he swooped in and saved her—no, she wouldn't think like that. He had been a complete boor, accusing her of not being a real farmer. Ha! He might be good-looking, but that was all. She wouldn't fall for a pretty face, that was for certain sure.

"Benjamin and I saw it from across the aisle," Naomi said. She grinned as she set down her glass of iced tea. "That man lifted her right out of the pen, like she weighed nothing. Sparks flew."

"Sparks did *not* fly," Amanda said. "Stop being *lecherich*."

"I'm not being ridiculous. I saw the look in your eyes."

Amanda pushed her half-empty plate away. "He tried to steal my goats out from under me. The least he could do after that was to catch me. If I had been falling. Which I wasn't. Not really."

Benjamin laughed. "Amanda, that man did not try to steal your goats from you. He was bidding, like everyone else."

"I have a plan for those goats. I need them."

Benjamin leaned back in his chair and studied her. "Maybe he did too."

"He didn't strike me as a serious farmer. I got a *gut* look at his hands. They weren't calloused enough."

"*Ya*, you got a *gut* look as he was saving you," Naomi said. She caught Miriam's eye and they both smiled.

Amanda wanted to yell at all of them. This conversation was not going in the direction she wanted. "Look, all I'm saying is that those goats needed to go to a serious farmer who is trying to make a living. They're top Angoras and I'm expanding our fiber production, so—"

"So, you didn't like him because he almost won the bid?" Leah asked from the doorway of the dining room. John stood beside her holding his baby, Abby, who looked tiny in his big arms. At six foot four inches, he towered over all of his in-laws.

"There you are," Amanda said. "You missed dinner."

"*Ya*, we couldn't get Abby to settle down, so we took her on a buggy ride," John said. "She's fast asleep now."

"Works every time," Leah said as she leaned into her husband and smiled. They had only been married for a few months, and she still lit up when she looked at him. Amanda wanted to roll her eyes every time she saw them together. She told herself it was because they were annoying, not because she was jealous.

"Don't let her change the subject on you, Leah," Miriam said. "You were just saying that Amanda is a bad winner."

Leah laughed. "That's not what I said."

"I'm translating to get to the point," Miriam said.

Amanda pushed back her chair and stood. "I'm going to check on the goats." She picked up her half-empty plate and carried it to the sink before slipping out of the room. The last thing she heard was Miriam murmuring something about how Amanda would push every suitor away if she weren't careful. "He wasn't a suitor!" Amanda shouted from the hallway, loudly enough to carry back into the dining room. "He was a stranger who tried to steal my goats!" The last thing she heard before storming out of the front door was the sound of laughter.

They didn't understand the feelings that were churning inside of her. She didn't understand herself. The man at the auction had been rude and condescending, responding with a grunt when she tried to joke with him. But the next time she saw him, he had wrapped his strong arms around her and pulled her to safety. Her heart had caught in her throat, her knees had gone weak, and she had lost herself in his blue eyes for a moment. Well, that had been silly of her. She would not think about *that* again.

Except that she was still thinking about it. And she could not stop.

The worst thing she could do would be to fall for a man who didn't support her dreams. It would make a mess of her life. She had been careful to guard her heart ever since she was old enough to be courted. She had to remain strong and independent in order to stay true to herself. She could not risk falling for a man, no matter how lonely she felt deep inside. She would not let her guard down now—and especially not for a man who clearly did not understand her. She would continue to follow her dreams, even though no one but L.D. would ever understand. And even though their relationship would never be anything more than a fantasy.

Amanda was resigned to being alone. In fact, she would fight tooth and nail to stay that way. Anything else was just too risky.

Chapter Two

Dear M.M.,

Nothing you say sounds silly to me. Why shouldn't you spend your time outside, doing what you love? I know that Amish women usually do the house-work, but I think you should do what you feel called to do. Why would Gott give you a love for farmwork if He wanted you to stay inside, doing the cooking and cleaning all day?

I need to be outdoors, too, so I understand. When I worked at the factory, I felt trapped. In the darkest months of the year, after a long ride in the hired Englisch van with the other men from my neighborhood, I used to clock in before the sun rose and clock out after it set. I ate lunch in a win-dowless break room, at a row of cafeteria tables. I missed the crunch of snow beneath my boots in the wintertime and the heat of the sun on my skin in the summertime. I missed having lunch with my family on the old picnic table beneath our oak tree, when my mamm piled our plates high with fried chicken, sauerkraut and slices of cold apple pie. I missed everything about the old farm.

So, I'm determined to make a go of my new farm. It's my one chance to make those memories real again. But starting up like this isn't easy. Thanks for all the support. Wish I had more time to write today, but I've got to repair the fence before the goats get out. They should always come first, ain't so?
Sincerely,
L.D.

David didn't want to admit to his family that he'd failed to get the goats he'd been determined to buy. His heart sank when his mother, father and little sister met him at the front door of their little farmhouse with eager eyes and wide smiles. He had to tell them that he had been outbid. As an Amish man, he wasn't supposed to be concerned with material wealth. But it was hard to come home empty-handed and stare into the faces of the people who counted on him, knowing that he was letting them down. He had convinced them that he could make this work, even though his father, Lloyd, had warned him that the risks of farming were too high, the profit margins too low. And now, as he checked and rechecked his accounting books every night, it looked like his father was right.

David took off his straw hat and turned it in his hands. "I didn't get them."

His mother's soft blue eyes crinkled at the corners as she gave him a genuine smile. "It's *oll recht*, David. *Gott* will provide."

"*Ya.*" David gave a curt nod. He knew that God would provide, but was afraid that it wouldn't be in the way that he wanted. What if it was God's will to provide for him through factory work, instead of fulfilling his dream of running his own farm? David shoved the thought away.

His ten-year-old sister, Katie, tugged on his sleeve. "Did you bring me back anything?" She had been a surprise blessing for the family, born sixteen years after David and long after their parents had given up hope of having a second child. David handed her a paper package of saltwater taffy that he had picked up at the auction food stand. "Sure did. Sorry it's not what you asked for, but I hope it'll do."

"*Danki*," Katie said as she grabbed the candy and tore open the translucent paper wrapping. "We already have lots of goats. I think I'd rather have candy, actually."

David chuckled and squeezed her thin shoulder. She was a skinny girl with freckles covering her face and arms, and a shy smile that lit up the room. "I'm glad," he said.

Lloyd smiled, but his eyes remained serious. He waited until David's mother, Lydia, and Katie headed toward the kitchen, then asked in a low voice, "How are the books looking, *sohn*?"

David cleared his throat and looked away. "Uh, you know, fine, I guess." His father had stopped working after an accident at the factory had left him with a permanent back injury. His mother managed to make a little extra money selling eggs and taking in sewing, but that didn't make ends meet. The entire family was depending on David.

Lloyd studied David for a moment before giving him a firm pat on the shoulder and turning away. David let out a sharp breath and shook his head. He was going to have to tell his father the full truth. The accounting wasn't adding up. They were losing too much money. This whole dream was about to slip away. But he wasn't quite ready to face that yet. He would talk to his father tomorrow morning, over coffee. First, he wanted to write to the only person who he could tell how he really felt.

David waited until the house was silent, the family's kerosene lanterns blown out for the night, the goats quiet in their shed. He sat down at the desk he had made with a couple of crates and an old board. It wasn't going to win any construction prizes, but it served its purpose. The green shade on his bedroom window was open, and moonlight filtered through the windowpanes, casting faint white light across the worn floorboards and the twin bed's simple metal frame. He readjusted his weight in the straight-backed chair and lit his kerosene lantern. The flame flickered and grew, lighting up the yellow notepad in front of him. He sighed and began to write, gripping the felt tip pen a little too tightly as the emotion spilled out.

Dear M.M.,
It's been a tough day. My flock isn't big enough to

He stopped, stared at the page, then crossed out the last sentence. He crumpled the paper and threw it into the wastebasket, then tried again.

Dear M.M.,
Farming is a good challenge. Any advice on how
to increase fiber production?

David reread the two sentences and nodded. That was better.

Too many people today aren't serious about farming. It's nice to be able to write to you for advice because I know you take it seriously and truly care about your livestock.

Was that too personal? No, it was okay because it was the truth. He admired M.M. for her dedication. She inspired him to keep going, even when he was discouraged. She had coaxed him through the early stages of raising goats, making sure he had the right equipment, followed all the steps correctly and kept his goats healthy. She knew far more than any of the books that he had checked out from the library. He hesitated, then decided to open up a little bit more.

You've really helped me out. I don't know what I would have done without you. Things aren't always easy.

An image of that Amanda woman flashed in his mind. She had not made things easy for him. She clearly had no idea what it was like to struggle or to need a little support. She had not even been appreciative when he saved her from falling on her head. He hadn't done it for a thank-you, but it would have been nice to get one. David shifted in his seat and forced his attention back on the letter.

It's good to have a friend who understands.
Sincerely,
L.D.

David sighed and set down the pen. He hoped that he hadn't gone too far, but he could not stop himself from reaching out to M.M. a little. Just as a friend. He knew that she wasn't married, but still, he didn't want to be too forward. She had been opening up to him more and more, so he figured it was okay to open up some too. It just felt natural.

An owl hooted outside as it swept past the house on silent wings. David glanced out the darkened window, then back to the letter. He folded it evenly and creased it carefully. He would mail it first thing in the morning. And maybe, if he was lucky, M.M. would mail him a letter right back. He sure hoped so. Because most days, David couldn't stop thinking about her. Maybe it was time for them to meet.

No.

He cut the thought off quickly. He didn't want to ruin a good thing. M.M. was supportive and helpful. She gave excellent advice. What if he messed that up? Better to keep things as they were than risk a meeting.

Even though his heart whispered otherwise.

The next morning, as David sipped his coffee at the kitchen table, Lloyd dropped a copy of *The Budget* newspaper in front of him. "Look here." Lloyd leaned over David's chair and stabbed a headline with his forefinger. "You should enter, *ya*?"

David scanned the first few lines of the article. There was going to be a big agricultural fair in Lancaster County.

"Before the registration deadline," Lloyd added when David didn't respond. "It's almost too late."

"*Ach*, I don't know, *Daed*."

"Enter what?" Katie asked as she grabbed the last cinnamon roll from a basket lined with red-checkered cloth.

"A livestock show," Lloyd said. He gave David a big clap on the back. "And our David here could win the blue ribbon with his goats, ain't so, *sohn*?"

David shifted in his seat. "There'll be a lot of *gut* entries."

"And yours will be the best," Lloyd said.

"Don't encourage him to pride," Lydia said as she strode into the dining nook with a fresh carafe of coffee.

"It isn't prideful to tell the truth," Lloyd said, then gave David a quick wink.

Lydia shook her head, but couldn't hide her smile.

David sighed. He didn't want to disappoint his father. "I've got *gut* goats, for certain sure. But they aren't producing milk like we need them to…"

"They're judging on looks. Your cashmeres and Angora goats look great. You wouldn't be entering your dairy goats."

David looked back down at the article. His mother topped off his mug with fresh black coffee as he read. Warm steam curled upward, bringing with it the smell of the dark roasted beans. The scent mingled with the cinnamon from the rolls his mother had baked that morning. These were the moments he had missed while working in the factory. There had not been time for quiet breakfasts together then. It had always been a hustle to get out the door and clock in on time, as if they were all *Englischers*. He used to nibble on his mother's cinnamon rolls while bumping across the countryside in the hired *Englisch* van, his first cup of coffee sloshing uncomfortably in his belly, his second one sealed in a metal thermos, ready for his lunch break.

David froze when he read a line that said Lancaster Fleece & Fiber would be on the judging panel at the fair. If they were there, then they would be looking for potential contracts. And if they noticed his goats and offered him a contract, then he would be all set. They were a big company that could give him a big contract. Finding good buyers for a niche local product wasn't always easy, especially for a small-time farmer like him. The cost of finishing the cashmere and mohair into yarn was too much for his little operation, so he needed to sell his fiber raw, in bulk. Up to now, he had been cobbling together his income from small sales that weren't sustainable. He also sold goat milk from his dairy goats, but that was mostly to local families who wanted fresh milk from a farm. None of it was enough to make ends meet.

David wanted to keep eating his meals in this little kitchen with its warm scents of coffee and cinnamon, the lingering smell of smoke from the woodstove, and the soft murmur of conversation from his parents and sister. Their bungalow-style farmhouse was smaller and older than the one he had grown up in, but it made a good home. They had been fortunate that it came with the farmland. The exterior paint was weathered, the blue-and-white kitchen linoleum was cracked and the blue wallpaper had faded to a soft gray, but that only added to the character. He didn't want to lose what he had here. Could this agricultural fair be the way to keep the farm going? A way to keep them in this cozy little home together? He looked up from the paper. "*Oll recht, Daed.* Maybe you're right. I'll look into it."

His mother set down the carafe and pulled out a chair at the compact dinette table. She slid into the seat and picked up the paper. "You'll have to talk to the bishop and make sure it's allowed. A lot of church districts would say it's too prideful to enter a contest."

"*Ya*," Lloyd said. "But I think he'll allow it."

David's heart began to pick up speed. This might work. And if it did, it could change everything. "You really think he will, *Daed*?"

"Sure. We're not as strict as Bluebird Hills or some of the other districts around here. It should be fine. Just keep in mind what's important and don't get too competitive. Remember why you're doing all of this." Lloyd nodded toward the goat shed outside and the rolling hills beyond.

Two days later, Amanda tucked L.D.'s latest letter into her wooden chest before heading out to the Bluebird Hills Feed & Seed. She had read and reread the lines enough to memorize them. The words rang in her head with every clip-clop of Clyde's big, steady hooves on the pavement. The sky shone a brilliant blue, with soft, wispy clouds that rode the warm breeze like white, rounded kites. Their shadows soared over the green fields and pastureland, racing the buggy along the back roads.

"It's good to have a friend who understands," Amanda murmured. This had been L.D.'s best letter yet. She could hardly believe he had written that. The short, simple sentence sang in her heart as the buggy rattled onward. She knew that the wheels were firmly planted on the pavement, but it felt as if she were floating. There was too much joy bubbling inside her to keep her on the ground. L.D. appreciated her. He valued her. He didn't tell her to spend more time baking and sewing so that she could be a good wife. He thought that she had plenty to offer, just the way she was.

Maybe she should invite him to Stoneybrook Farm. Then she could finally see him. They could talk face-to-face, and then maybe...

Amanda frowned. And then maybe *what*? They would live happily-ever-after, like an *Englisch* fairy tale? Amanda's hands tightened around the leather reins. This was real life. What if meeting L.D. ruined it all? What if he didn't like her? What if *she* didn't like *him*? What if this was just a dream she had created and enjoyed *because* it was a dream? Reality could pop it like a soap bubble. In real life, L.D. might not be the hero he portrayed in his letters. It was easy for a man to appreciate a woman's wisdom from afar, but it was different when it came to courting. He might feel threatened and insecure then.

Not that they would be courting. Amanda grimaced. She was being presumptuous. He might not even be interested in her in that way. He had specified *friend* in his letter. What exactly did *friend* mean? She analyzed the word the rest of the way into town, agonizing over whether it was an invitation to get closer, or a statement that they were *just* friends.

Love was so confusing.

Amanda flinched. She wasn't in love. She was in *like*. She couldn't be in love with a man she had never met. Even if her heart did jump into her throat every time a letter arrived and his words warmed her for days after. She had to remind herself that he was a fantasy, and that was all. She didn't even know what he looked like.

But didn't that make it even more romantic?

Amanda's frown deepened as she turned onto Main-street. She needed to stop thinking about this. She passed the row of old-fashioned storefronts that looked like a postcard out of the 1950s. *Englisch* tourists sat at wrought iron tables on the sidewalk in front of the coffee shop, sipping from cardboard cups and chatting. An Amish family was walking into the hardware store next door. She heard the bell chime and the hearty hello from the shopkeeper. Amanda loved the hardware store. It had been in Bluebird Hills forever and felt like a time capsule inside, with its faint scent of metal and grease, its worn wooden floors and wooden shelves filled with miscellaneous odds and ends. Not like the chain hardware stores with their jarring fluorescent lights and high warehouse ceilings.

At the end of the block sat Beiler's Quilt and Fabric Shop, stocked with plain, solid-colored fabric and Amish-made quilts that sold on consignment. A handful of buggies were parked in the small lot beside the yellow-and-white building. The horses waited patiently, flicking their tails to discourage flies. Amanda slowed and looked both ways at the stop sign, then slapped the reins. "Walk on," she said and Clyde leaned into the harness, jerking the buggy forward.

Across the street sat a square, brick building painted white. A faded wooden sign with the words *FEED & SEED* stretched across the front. Amanda steered Clyde into a parking space designed for Amish buggies. "Whoa," she said and tugged the reins. Clyde whinnied and shook his head, and the buggy shuddered to a stop. Amanda hopped out and patted Clyde on the neck before tethering him to the hitching post. She had a spring in her step and a smile on her face as she strode through the doors and into the well-worn store. Her great-grandparents had bought their farm supplies here decades ago, before automobiles competed with buggies for parking and when the only sounds coming from the streets were the soft, steady beat of horse hooves and the jangle of harnesses.

Now *Englisch* engines growled down Mainstreet, but inside the store it felt as if nothing had changed from a time when everyone had lived as simply as the Amish. Sure, there were electric lights and heating, and a fancy cash register, but the interior was still lined with worn wooden boards, and the floors were covered in stacks of burlap sacks that filled the space with a familiar, earthy smell. Beside the counter sat a big wooden barrel stuffed with old-fashioned penny candy. And, perhaps best of all, the *Englischer* shopkeeper, Billy Tyler, knew her family and exactly what she needed. His grandfather had opened the store over a hundred years ago. Billy and Amanda always stopped and chatted about what a gallon of goat's milk or a bushel of corn was going for these days.

Amanda was headed over to say hello to him when she stopped short. There, beside a shelf stocked with live-stock vitamins, stood the man from the auction. Amanda wrinkled her nose. She wanted to sweep past and ignore him. He had insulted her after the auction, acting as if she was just a hobby farmer. He had not taken her seriously.

But he had also saved her from a fall, even if she didn't want to admit it. And, after his strong hands had locked around her waist, his eyes had met hers, and she had not been able to pull away from that blue-eyed gaze.

Well, that was silly. Of course she could pull away

from him. She was still annoyed with him for his attitude. It was nice that he had rescued her, but she hadn't asked for the help. And plenty of men had eyes like that. There was no reason to get weak in the knees over him. Not that she was getting weak in the knees. She would absolutely not feel that way about him. He was not the type of man who would ever appreciate her.

The man glanced up. She saw the flicker of recognition pass over his face before his expression clamped down and she couldn't read his emotions. He gave a polite nod, without smiling, then looked back down at the package on the wooden shelf in front of him. Amanda knew that she should keep walking. But she couldn't. She tried. She really did. But she had to prove that she knew what she was doing.

"*Ach*, those aren't the best vitamins," she said as she sauntered past. "You should try that brand." She pointed toward another package on the shelf. She kept her demeanor calm and casual. She would show him that she was a real farmer.

"Oh." The man frowned as he glanced from the package in his hand to the one on the shelf. "Alright."

Amanda was surprised. She had not expected that response. "You're not going to question whether or not I know what I'm doing?"

"I guess that depends on if you do or not. *Do* you know what you're doing?"

"Of course I do," Amanda snapped. "But you clearly don't. That brand has added fillers. The other one doesn't."

The man gave a sly smile. "Maybe I like fillers."

"Maybe you do, but your goats sure don't."

The man paused and scratched his jawline. "You know, you're the one who won, right? I lost. Shouldn't I be the one who's bent out of shape about it, instead of you?"

"I am not bent out of shape."

The man raised an eyebrow. "You sure about that?"

"I was offering advice. I was being nice, ain't so?"

The man grunted and turned his attention back to the package on the shelf in front of him.

Amanda couldn't let it go. "I have every right to be annoyed."

The man sighed, then looked back at her. "Why? There's no need to gloat. I lost a lot when you won that bid."

"And I would have lost a lot, too, if you had won. Why should your farm matter more than mine?"

The man's expression tightened. "Because—"

"Because I'm just a hobby farmer who keeps goats as pets?"

"That wasn't what I was going to say."

"It was what you were thinking. Even though you know nothing about me."

The man's jaw clenched, then unclenched. "Look, I shouldn't have made that comment to you at the auction, the one about the pet goats."

Amanda gave a firm nod of victory.

The man looked at her with an even, steady gaze. "You know, you could apologize for gloating."

Amanda blinked a few times. "You didn't apologize, but you expect me to?"

"I just apologized."

"*Nee*, you said that you shouldn't have done something. That's not the same as apologizing."

The man took a deep breath of air and let it out sharply.

"You didn't say you were sorry," Amanda said when the man didn't respond.

"I'm sorry." The words came out through gritted teeth.

"You don't sound very sorry."

"Doing my best here, okay? Can you try to meet me halfway?"

Amanda pursed her lips and stared at the man. He was right. She *had* gloated at the auction. It had felt good to show him that she knew what she was doing. It had felt good to win. She liked showing others that she was competent. Especially when men looked at her small stature and treated her with condescension, as if she were not much more capable than a child. She often got the feeling that they wanted to pat her on the head and send her on her way.

But still, she knew that she should not have gloated. Even if the man had it coming.

"Fine. I'm sorry I gloated."

"Now who's the one who doesn't sound sorry?"

"Great minds think alike."

The man gave a sly smile. "So, you think I have a great mind, huh?"

Amanda scowled at him. "You know what I mean."

"Look, maybe we can call a truce and start over. From the beginning." The man flashed a mischievous grin. "You know, before you stole my goats."

Amanda started to argue, but realized that he was teasing her. She returned the smile. "You mean after you tried to steal *my* goats."

"Yeah." The man held her gaze for a moment. Their eyes locked and Amanda felt a funny feeling inside her belly. She realized that she liked talking to this man. Which didn't make any sense at all.

Then the man tore his gaze away and cleared his throat. He shifted his weight from one foot to the other. "So, uh, you know which vitamins are best?"

"*Ya.* Sure do."

"That brand?" He pointed toward the package that Amanda had indicated earlier.

"What kind of goats are you raising?"

"Cashmeres and Angoras."

"Then that is the best one for you. It'll really put a shine into their coats."

The man smiled. "Perfect. I need to get them looking as *gut* as possible for the livestock fair."

Amanda froze as soon as his words registered. "The livestock fair here in Lancaster County?"

"*Ya.*"

"You're going to show them?"

"*Ya.*"

"Oh." Amanda felt her guard go back up. This man was competition.

He watched her reaction. "What? Is there a problem with the show?"

"*Ya.* There is."

The man frowned. "What is it?"

"I'm entering too."

The man raised his eyebrows, then let out a long, low whistle. "*Vell*, may the best man—or woman—win."

"You stole my line."

The man tipped his straw hat, grinned at her and sauntered past. He scooped up the package of vitamins as he walked by. "*Danki* for the tip," he said without looking back.

Amanda clenched her fists. She watched him casually stroll to the counter, set the package down and make small talk with Billy. He was cutting into her territory, her world. He did not belong here. And now he was the one gloating—after *she* had apologized!

Now she really had to win that livestock competition. She would show him what she was made of, that was certain sure.

Chapter Three

Dear L.D.,
Some people say I'm too confident. Or even a lit-
tle combative. But I just want everyone to see that
I know what I'm doing. Is that too much to ask?
Good to know I have a friend who understands
me and sees that I'm capable. That helps a lot.
Your friend,
M.M.

David felt like he understood M.M. Amanda, on the other hand, was a mystery. He didn't know what to make of her. But he did know that he liked the confident sparkle in her brown eyes. He liked teasing her and watching them sparkle even brighter. He even liked her sharp, witty retorts. She was smart, that was certain sure. He had gotten an unexpected flutter of butterflies in his stomach when their eyes had locked.

But she was also as defensive as a cornered snake, as far as he could tell. Better to keep his distance.

David paid the shopkeeper and headed toward the door when he heard a thudding noise, followed by a grunt. He turned to see Amanda struggling to lift a big bag of goat feed. He stared for a moment, sighed and headed toward her. He hoped this wasn't going to be a mistake, but what choice did he have? He couldn't just walk out and let her lift that bag by herself. And maybe a small part of him wanted to show her that he could do something she couldn't, after all her gloating. He wanted her to see that he wasn't so useless after all, even if he didn't know the best vitamin brand for Angora goats or have the cash to outbid her at an auction.

As he crossed the store, David watched Amanda strain to lift the bag, let go and reposition her arms. She grunted and tried again, but the bag only shifted a little.

"Having some trouble?" David asked.

Amanda dropped the bag and turned around to glare at him. "I'm doing fine."

David smiled. "Doesn't look like it."

"Who's the one gloating now?" Amanda glared at him for another beat before turning her attention back to the bag.

"I got this," David said as he swooped past her, scooped up the bag and heaved it onto his shoulder. "I'll walk it up front for you."

"*Nee*, I've got it."

"Actually, looks like I do." David patted the bag with his free hand, then headed toward the front of the store, balancing the bag on his shoulder. No wonder Amanda couldn't lift it. The bag was heavier than he had anticipated, barely manageable for a man his size. There was no way someone as small as her could handle it. He gritted his teeth and tried to look nonchalant. He would never let her know that he was struggling under the weight.

Amanda grunted and followed behind him. He

couldn't see her expression, but he could certainly imagine it. David was enjoying the situation more than he should. He liked looking like a hero. He didn't get to experience that very often.

"I don't need any help," Amanda mumbled as she trailed behind him.

"You sure about that?" David gave a sly little grin and stopped walking. "I could just set it back down on the floor, if you want to take it from here." He turned around to face her. "Or I could just hand it to you?" He made an exaggerated movement as if he were about to drop the bag into her arms. He was not going to, of course. He was just teasing her.

Amanda gave him a sharp look. "*Nee*, you've already carried it this far. May as well keep going."

David's grin widened. "May as well." He gave her a wink before turning around and strolling to the checkout counter. He could hear her footsteps padding behind him. He was enjoying this too much. He had to remind himself that he shouldn't try to have fun with her. She was a rival, after all. And she didn't seem to mind staying that way. Well, he could be just as competitive as her.

He dropped the bag onto the counter with a heavy thump.

"Good to see you, Amanda," the man behind the counter said. He wore a plaid flannel shirt rolled up at the sleeves and looked to be in his sixties, with salt-and-pepper hair and a generous midsection. He nodded toward David, then smiled at Amanda. "You going to introduce me to your friend? You two courting?"

"Absolutely not," Amanda said quickly.

"We're just friends," David added.

"Competitors," Amanda said.

The shopkeeper raised his eyebrows.

David cleared his throat. "Right. Competitors."

"Billy, this is…" Amanda frowned. "What is your name?"

David chuckled. "Didn't think to ask me yet, ain't so?" He met Billy's eyes, nodded and said, "David Troyer."

Billy returned the nod as he rang up the package. David and Amanda stood in awkward silence. "That'll be 42.37," Billy said.

Amanda handed him two twenties and a five.

"You going to show your goats at the livestock fair?" Billy asked as he slid the bills into the cash register drawer.

"*Ya*," David and Amanda answered simultaneously.

Billy chuckled. "I see. Now I get it." He handed Amanda her change, then looked at David. "She'll be tough to beat."

Amanda beamed.

"I'm beginning to get that impression," David said.

"Yep. She's been coming here since she was a newborn baby. Her parents used to bring her in when they shopped. And her grandparents used to shop here, when my father owned the place." Billy leaned his hip against the counter and crossed his arms. "Haven't seen you around here before."

"I don't live nearby. Just happened to be passing through today. Made sense to stop in here instead of making an extra trip to my local feed and seed."

"What brought you to town?" Billy asked.

"Dropping off a pie that my mother made for a cousin who's been ailing lately."

Amanda narrowed her eyes. "You probably rescue kittens too."

David chuckled. "I've been known to do that."

"Humph." Amanda tugged the bag of feed toward her. It slid across the counter in slow, jerky motions. "I'm not fooled."

"Let me get that for you," Billy said. "I'll carry it to your buggy."

"No need," David said. "I've got it." He lifted the bag before either the shopkeeper or Amanda could argue.

"Competitors, you say?" Billy said, then laughed softly.

Amanda pretended that she didn't hear him.

"Lead the way," David said. "You parked out front?"

Amanda sighed. "*Ya.*" She threw Billy a quick wave. "See you."

He nodded as he touched the brim of his frayed baseball cap.

David followed Amanda into the bright afternoon sunlight. The bell chimed as the door creaked open, then shut behind him. "You could just say *danki*, you know."

"And you could stop trying to show me up."

"Is that what you think I'm doing?"

"I don't know you. This could all be a ploy to convince me to let my guard down, to get to know my secrets so that you can win the competition."

"That's ridiculous."

"Is it? You're leaving here with the vitamins that I recommended. Otherwise, your Angoras would have had a duller coat on fair day."

"That was a *gut* coincidence that went in my favor."

"Anyway, it's obvious that you're gloating." She

crossed her arms. "Poor little Amanda, barely five feet tall," she said in a mocking tone. "Can't even carry a bag of goat feed."

"*Vell*, can you?" David stared down at her as a smile tugged on his lips.

Amanda stared back, arms still crossed.

"I'll take that as a no."

Amanda's lips tightened into a thin line.

David walked around to the back of the buggy and dropped the feed bag inside, sending up a cloud of dust. He straightened up and stretched his back. "You got someone to unload that for you when you get home?"

"I'll be fine."

David nodded. He knew he should walk away, but he couldn't resist. "You sure about that? You're not much bigger than that bag is."

"That's a huge exaggeration."

David shrugged. "I don't know if *huge* is the right word here."

Amanda jutted out her chin. "I might be small, but I'm completely capable."

"Maybe not completely." He nodded toward the feed bag.

"I would have managed if you hadn't come along."

"Debatable. Hey, have you ever tried hitching one of your goats up to a little cart, like children do sometimes? You know, to haul stuff around for you. Maybe that would help."

Amanda made a noise in the back of her throat that sounded mighty close to a growl. She stormed around to the front of the buggy without giving him another look.

"I guess we'll settle this at the fair," David said as she untied her horse from the hitching post.

Amanda spun around to face him. "Oh, we'll settle this all right. Then you'll see exactly what I'm capable of."

David raised his hands in mock surrender. "Whoa, now. You're making me nervous."

Amanda stalked to the side of the buggy and climbed inside. "Just you wait. You're going to see exactly how good I am at what I do. And you won't be laughing anymore." Her eyes flashed as she slapped the reins.

David let out a long, slow breath as he watched her pull out of the parking space. He wasn't sure what he had gotten himself into, but he did know that he wanted to win the competition more than ever now.

Amanda marched straight over to the bishop's house as soon as she got home from the Feed & Seed. Amos Yoder and his wife, Edna, lived next door to Stoneybrook Farm. Amanda and her siblings had grown up playing in their sunflower field, running through their orchards and swimming in their lake. Plus, Benjamin's wife, Emma, was Amos' niece, so the families were particularly close. Even so, Amanda had put off asking the bishop because she feared what his answer would be. And now, the contest was only a few days away.

Her stomach churned uncomfortably as she trotted through the gate and down the grassy hill to the Yoders' side yard. Bees buzzed around Edna's tidy kitchen garden, which stretched the width of the farmhouse. The butterflies in Amanda's stomach fluttered harder as she rounded the corner and trotted up the front porch steps.

Some church districts might say that it was too prideful to compete in a contest. *Most* districts, if she were honest with herself.

Amanda squared her shoulders and rapped on the door. Not her district, surely. She had to compete. She had to beat David—Amanda caught herself. That was a very un-Amish thought. Maybe she wasn't approaching this situation the right way. But then she remembered the expression of superiority on David's face when he implied that she wasn't a serious farmer, and the doubt evaporated.

She would not let him win.

The door swung open and Edna appeared in the threshold, wiping her hands on her apron. A few strands of gray hair had come undone beneath her *kapp*, and her plump cheeks were red. "*Ach*, Amanda, I'm glad to see you! I've been canning all day and I'm ready for a rest. I'll pour us some *kaffi, ya*?"

"You should have had a work frolic," Amanda said as she wiped her shoes on the mat and followed Edna inside. "We would have *kumme* over to help."

Edna waved Amanda into the living room. "No need. There wasn't a lot to put up. And I enjoy the work." Edna grinned. "But I suppose I'm not as young as I used to be. It takes more out of me nowadays."

"At least let me help you with the *kaffi*."

"I already have a pot on," Edna said.

Amanda hesitated in the doorway. Maybe this wasn't such a good idea. Was she asking something outlandish? It had seemed reasonable when it was just a thought in her head, but now she felt sheepish. Amish folks shouldn't try to stand out or get attention. "Um, actually, I was here to see Amos." Amanda hesitated, then added quickly, "But I'd love to visit with you too, of course."

Edna's brow crinkled. "Is everything *oll recht*?"

Amanda forced a smile. She ignored the lump in her throat. "*Ya*, of course. Everything's fine."

Edna gave one of her motherly smiles. "*Vell*, I'll pour *kaffi* for three and let him know you're here."

"*Danki.*"

Amanda slipped into the living room to wait. A black potbellied stove filled the small space with heat and the scent of woodsmoke. Edna's quilts lay folded on the back of the couch and on a quilt rack beside a wicker rocking chair. The room looked neat and organized, everything swept clean and spotless. Amanda leaned over the elaborate double-nine-patch quilt and ran her finger over the stitching. Perfectly even. Amanda sighed and moved to the window. She could see the peach and pear orchards in the distance, standing in rows like soldiers at attention. The pond sparkled behind the trees, nestled between the rolling hills.

The afternoon sun shone through the panes, highlighting the fact that there wasn't a streak on the glass or a speck of dust on the windowsill. Edna's house was pristine. Amanda knew that Edna enjoyed the work. She always said that it satisfied her and made her feel a sense of daily accomplishment. Amanda wished she could feel that way. She so badly wanted to enjoy keeping house. Life would be so much easier if she could. There would be plenty of suitors, then a house full of babies, if she were just willing to swallow her dreams and be someone other than herself.

"Hello there," Amos said from the doorway.

Amanda spun around and smiled. Amos always made her feel better, no matter how low she was. His sharp nose, rosy cheeks and wizened expression reminded her of a jovial gnome, especially when he had a cheerful twinkle in his eye. He was a small man, which only highlighted how big and welcoming his personality was. "It's good to see you, Amanda. Everything *oll recht*?"

"*Ach, ya.* Of course." Amanda swallowed hard. The churning in her stomach told her everything was *not* all right. It felt like her future was on the line right now. But that was silly. This was only a contest. Except it seemed like much, much more than that. It was a chance to prove herself. And to show up David, if she admitted it. Well, she didn't want to admit that to herself, and certainly not to the bishop.

Edna swept in with a tray of coffee and gingersnap cookies. Amanda fumbled a little when she took a cup. Edna and Amos glanced at one another, then smiled at her. "Why don't you tell me what's bothering you?" Amos asked. Edna gave an encouraging nod as she settled into the rocking chair.

Amanda sank onto the couch and forced herself to return their smiles. She was beginning to feel foolish. What would they think about such a prideful request? And how could she explain that it went much deeper than just wanting to win? She couldn't even explain it to herself, really. She just knew that she longed to be recognized and valued, and she felt like winning this contest would give her that. It would fill a need that she couldn't quite name.

Amanda let out a deep breath. "*Vell*, I was hoping, um…" She shifted in her seat.

Edna and Amos leaned closer. Amanda knew that she was about to disappoint them. She should be seeking humility, not recognition.

"There's an opportunity for me to help the farm." There, that was a good way to explain it. And it was the truth. Or at least part of the truth. There *would* be plenty of buyers at the show and they would be looking for the best fiber.

"Go on," Amos said.

Edna took a sip of coffee without taking her eyes off Amanda.

"You know that there's going to be a big agricultural fair, right?"

"Sure."

"*Ya*, and..." Amanda cleared her throat. The room felt much hotter than it had been when she'd walked in. "*Vell*, there is going to be a livestock show and I was hoping that I could show my goats." She bit her lip, then added quickly, "You know, so the buyers can see what we've got to offer. It could help us get more contracts."

"You want to compete?" Amos asked.

"*Ya.*" Amanda's heart was in her throat. It felt so wrong to say it when asked directly like that.

A wrinkle appeared between Amos's brows. He leaned back in his chair and slowly ran his fingers through his long, white beard. "And you want to win, ain't so?"

Amanda knew the answer was obvious. "*Ya*," she said quietly. "I want to win."

Amos sighed. "You're a hard worker, Amanda."

"*Ya.*" Edna nodded. "A hard worker."

"And that's a *gut* thing," Amos said. His voice was gentle, but firm. "But we don't work for recognition."

Amanda's stomach dropped. He was going to say no. Everything in her wanted to argue and plead her case, but she managed to hold it in.

Amos stood up. "Let me show you something." He motioned toward the door, then led her to the front porch, grabbing his straw hat from a peg on the wall before heading outside. Edna followed behind and they all stood side by side, looking out at the pastures and fields that surrounded the house. Amos pointed to the farms in the distance. "What do you notice about them?" he asked.

"They all look alike," Amanda said. The buildings seemed small and far away, scattered among the green hills. The white silos and white barns looked like matching children's toys, all from the same set.

"That's right." Amos moved his pointer finger to the farms across the highway. "And what about those?"

Amanda studied the *Englischer* houses and barns. "They're all different." Some of the barns were red, some of the silos silver. One house was beige with a bright red door and red shutters. Another house was painted blue.

"The *Englisch* try to stand out, to outdo one another. They want to be seen and noticed. But we try to be like one another. No one stands out. No one tries to be better than their neighbor. Does that make sense?"

It did and it didn't. Amanda understood the principle— she had heard it all her life—and yet, she still longed to be seen for who she was. An individual. She was not exactly like everyone else. Not even close. She couldn't get her voice to say yes, but she managed to nod.

Edna patted Amanda's shoulder. They were being so nice about telling her no that it made Amanda feel bad. She shouldn't want the recognition. A good Amish person wouldn't. But she couldn't stop that need inside of her, crying out for validation.

"So, I can't allow you to enter a contest," Amos said. "It isn't in line with our faith. But you can still go to the agricultural show, as long as you don't compete. If it's *Gott*'s will for you to find a buyer, He will still put them in your path. You can't stop His will."

Amanda nodded again. She knew that was true. The Amish believed that God was always in control. But that didn't stop her from wanting to express herself, to show everyone that she was Amanda—not a copy of her neighbor. But she did not tell Amos or Edna that. She forced herself to smile, as she always did, and hide what she felt inside.

She waited until she got back home, to the privacy of her own bedroom, before she broke down in tears.

Amanda gave herself a good twenty minutes to cry. Then she poured water from the porcelain pitcher into the basin, washed her face and smoothed her dress. It was time to *do* something about the situation. But what could she do? She could not go against the bishop. Amanda sank down onto her bed and hugged her knees to her chest. The mattress springs creaked beneath her weight. A goat bleated from the farmyard, and distant footsteps thudded from somewhere in the house.

There was only one person she could turn to at a time like this. The thought sent a warm wave of relief through her. What if she overcame this disappointment by bringing something good into her life? She could get over the loss if she replaced it with something better.

L.D. was something better. He understood her. He made her feel like she had nothing to prove. What if she took the plunge and suggested they meet? Amanda released her knees and sat up straight. Anticipation zipped through her. Could she do that? Her heart beat hard and fast at the thought.

No. It was too forward. Too risky. But maybe there was a way... Amanda stood up and walked to her desk. Her writing paper lay in a disordered stack beside her pen, waiting for her. She took a deep breath and cracked her knuckles. She needed to get this right. Not too obvious, but not so subtle that L.D. failed to get the point.

Amanda uncapped the pen and stared at the blank page. Sunlight streamed through the window and warmed her face. Her eyes moved to the sweeping vista of pastureland beyond her second-story bedroom. The green grass looked bright and fresh in the sunshine. Her goats grazed on the hillside and she watched two of the kids kick up their feet and butt one another. Amanda smiled. She knew exactly what to do. She would suggest that L.D. visit a goat farm—the biggest farm in the county. But she wouldn't say it was hers. She would dangle the hint and hope he caught on—or that he still showed up even if he didn't get the hint.

After ten minutes and three rewrites, Amanda chewed the tip of her pen as she read over the letter. She nodded and smiled. She wasn't risking complete humiliation, or the loss of their friendship. It was just enough to nudge L.D. to Stoneybrook Farm, without being too forward.

If this worked, she just might meet the man of her dreams—and find a future together that would bring far more fulfillment than winning a competition.

Chapter Four

Dear M.M.,
It's hard to feel like no one appreciates you. I feel
the same way, sometimes. If my farm isn't successful, I'm afraid everyone will think that I didn't work
hard enough. I have a big opportunity coming up
that might make the difference between success
and failure, but I'm afraid I won't be good enough.
There's still so much that I don't know. And there's
so much we can't control when it comes to farming.
Goats have minds of their own, ain't so?
Your friend,
L.D.

David's last letter to M.M. had been risky. He had
opened up to her and admitted that he was afraid of
failure. It felt good to tell someone how much pressure
he was under to succeed. He felt lighter, freer now, as
if he weighed a little bit less, or gravity wasn't quite as
powerful. He hadn't told her everything, of course. He
didn't want her to know that he was planning on showing his goats at the agricultural fair. What if she thought
he wasn't ready? That would be humiliating.

Now, after two days of waiting, he had received a response. David stood beside the mailbox as he tore open
the envelope and read M.M.'s new letter. After he finished, he refolded the letter and exhaled. She had suggested that he visit goat farms in the area to see other
strategies firsthand. She didn't invite him to *her* farm
specifically. But he wondered if that was what she was
hoping he would do. Could this be a subtle way of suggesting that they meet? His heart thudded into his throat
at the thought. He tugged at his collar. Had it been this
tight a few minutes ago?

No, that couldn't be right. She had not told him her
address. He only had the PO box to go by, which told
him nothing. He double-checked the return address on
the envelope. Still the same PO box. He frowned and
told himself to stop being silly. Of course this wasn't
an invitation to meet her. She only saw him as a friend.

And who knew who she really was, anyway? She
could be anybody. If they ever did meet in person, it
could ruin everything. Was that a risk he was willing to
take? Well, it didn't matter, because she had not given
him the option. This was her chance to invite him to her
farm and she had not. He frowned as he reread the letter.

Wait.

He read the line a third time.

*Stoneybrook Farm is the biggest goat farm in
the county. You could start there.*

Could that be her farm? Was this a veiled invitation
to meet? David took off his straw hat and ran his fingers
through his hair. He had heard of Stoneybrook Farm,

but only vaguely. He knew it was big and was run by an Amish family—a bunch of sisters and brothers, maybe. He couldn't quite remember. If he were *Englisch*, he would look it up on the internet right now. Instead, he could only wonder.

Well, there was *something* he could do.

David's stomach tightened. Could he? Of course he could. But *should* he? He let out a long, slow breath. What if he went to Stoneybrook Farm and she didn't like him? Or what if she wasn't who he had imagined her to be?

David frowned. This was an exercise in foolishness. That probably wasn't a veiled invitation at all. It was just a good suggestion. Why would she want to meet him? Why would she feel as strongly about him as he did about her? She had never said anything about wanting to take things further. It was perfectly logical that she would encourage him to visit the biggest goat farm in the county. Why read more into it?

He kept trying to convince himself of that as he milked his goats, then spread out a new bed of hay in the goat shed. But the thought of meeting M.M. was too powerful to ignore. Now that he had the hope, he could not extinguish it. Sure, she might not be at Stoneybrook Farm. And if she were, she might not have feelings for him. Or he might not end up having feelings for her. Although he found that hard to imagine. But either way, it was worth the risk.

The realization shot through him like a flame. He set down the pitchfork. He had to know. He had to take the chance.

Ten minutes later, David had his horse hitched up to the buggy and was climbing aboard. His mother poked her head out of the front door as he pulled the hand brake. "Where are you off to in such a hurry?" she asked.

"*Ach*, just need to run an errand." David felt his face flush. He felt like he was sneaking around to meet a secret girlfriend, which was ridiculous. M.M. probably didn't even live at Stoneybrook Farm. But his heart desperately hoped she did. He knew because it was beating so fast that it felt like it might fly right out of his chest.

"Will you be home for lunch?"

"*Nee*, go on and eat without me." Stoneybrook Farm was about as far away as an Amish horse and buggy could reasonably travel. M.M. had given him the address in her letter, in case he followed her advice. He swallowed hard. That did feel like a mighty big hint. Maybe she really did want him to visit, so he could find her there. "I've got to go," he said as he slapped the reins. He couldn't bear to wait another minute.

It was the longest buggy ride of his life. He barely noticed the rolling green hills, the patchwork of golden-yellow fields or the white barns and silos. When he passed a flock of goats nibbling grass behind a fence that ran alongside the highway, he didn't even give them a second look. His mind was focused on one thing and one thing only. By the time he reached the outskirts of Bluebird Hills, his jaw and shoulders ached. He had not realized how tense he was until then.

He scanned the highway until he saw a big wooden sign at the end of a long gravel driveway: *Stoneybrook Farm. Fresh goat milk and goat milk soap for sale.* He tugged the reins to the right, and the horse turned and plodded onward, up the sloping hill. The buggy wheels crunched on the gravel as he wound along the narrow driveway. To the right, he saw a tidy farm with peach and pear orchards behind a white clapboard house. A big kitchen garden filled the side yard.

The buggy looped around a hill and a bigger farmhouse appeared, this time on his left. The home had a double front porch—one on top of the other—and additions that had been tacked on, somewhat haphazardly, to the original structure. It looked well-worn and well loved, and large enough to house a big extended family. A weathered, unpainted barn sat across the farmyard from the house. The space in between bustled with activity as chickens pecked the earth, a goose waddled back and forth like a sentinel on duty, and a big, brindle-colored dog lounged in the shade of an oak tree. A red wheelbarrow stood near an empty goat pen. David scanned the hill that sloped upward from behind the house. He could make out a herd of goats in the distance, foraging in a faraway pasture.

The dog's ears pricked up and he raised his head as the buggy approached the gate. When David hopped out to unhitch the latch, the dog leaped to his feet and barked. The front door of the farmhouse opened and David's breath caught in his chest. A woman appeared. She raised her hand to her forehead and squinted into the sun to stare at him.

For a moment, David refused to believe what he was seeing. It couldn't be. It just couldn't. Of all the things that he had imagined happening when he finally met M.M., this was the one he had never thought of.

Amanda stared into the sun as she hovered in the doorway. She couldn't make out who was beside the buggy, but she knew it was a stranger. She didn't recognize the horse. Could it be L.D.? Amanda's heart dropped into her stomach before zipping back into her chest. She swallowed hard and smoothed her apron. She had been hoping all day that he would appear. And all day she had been telling herself to stop dreaming. Yes, she had hinted in the letter that he should visit her, but she wasn't sure that he would get the hint. And, if he did, she wasn't sure that he would come. What if he didn't want to meet her?

But he was here. It had to be him. It just *had* to be.

She grinned, flew out of the door and raced down the front porch steps, her bare feet pounding across the wooden boards. She was finally going to meet the man she had dreamed of for so long. Everything in her life had led up to this moment. It was time. Finally, she would not be alone anymore. The man who understood her would be more than just words on a page.

As she drew closer, the buggy blocked the sun, and his face suddenly came into view. Something slow and terrible registered in her brain. Her chest constricted. She could not quite believe it for a moment.

The man beside the buggy was David, her rival. The man who represented all the hurt and rejection that haunted her. She thought that meeting him would offset the disappointment from missing the competition. Instead, she had been plunged into a far deeper disappointment. This was an absolute calamity.

Amanda sputtered to a stop. "What are you doing here?" she managed to ask. It was all some kind of mistake. This was not L.D. It couldn't be. David was here for another reason. *Please, please, please let him be here for another reason*, she prayed silently, through gritted teeth.

His face looked as disturbed and crestfallen as she imagined hers must. "I…uh…" He rubbed his hand across his face, as if he couldn't quite bear to be there, in that moment. "I got a letter suggesting I come…"

"*Nee.*" Amanda shook her head, hard. "That can't be."

David's face flicked back to life and he smiled. "*Ach, gut.* For a second, I thought…" He shook his head. "Never mind. It wasn't you."

"Wasn't me who sent the letter?"

"*Ya.*"

Amanda squared her shoulders and tried to push away the shock and disappointment searing through her. "*Nee,* I sent the letter. I meant that it can't be *you.*" She shook her head. "Of all the people in world…"

David squeezed his eyes shut and pinched the bridge of his nose. "*Recht.* Of all the people." He dropped his hand and opened his eyes. "I don't know what to say."

Amanda put her hands on her hips. "*Vell,* you can start by explaining yourself. Why didn't you tell me your name was David in your letters?"

"Why didn't you tell me your name was Amanda?"

"I asked first." She didn't want to admit that he had a good point.

"Most folks call me Lloyd's David, or L.D. for short." He looked away. "Folks I'm close to, anyway."

Amanda felt a little stab go through her heart. He had felt close to her. Just like she had to him. She pushed the emotion away. "So, you're not the only David in the family."

"*Ya.*"

"Same with my brother's son. He's Benjamin too, but we don't call him Benjamin's Benjamin. It's too long…"

Amanda realized that she was about to tell David about her family. Now that she knew David was actually L.D., she felt an unexpected ability to talk to him, as if she had known him a long time. Well, she had, in a way. She would have to resist that urge. It made her feel strange and confused. Amanda cut herself off. "Never mind."

David raised his eyebrows. "So what about M.M.? What's the story there?"

Amanda frowned. "It doesn't matter."

"Hmm. So you don't want me to know. Interesting." David gave a sly smile. "Hiding something?"

David's smile seemed so engaging and playful that Amanda was tempted to answer him. She crossed her arms instead.

"Hey, Mini Manda!" Benjamin's voice shouted from across the farmyard.

David's smile widened to a grin. "Mini Manda." His eyes moved to her feet, then back to her eyes. "I see. Or actually I don't—because there isn't much to see. You know, since you're mini-sized."

Amanda turned to see Benjamin trotting past the chicken coop and coming toward them. She threw him a scowl before turning back to David. "I am at least five feet."

David gave her a look.

"Okay. I'm nearly five feet. That is only four inches below average."

"Nearly five feet, huh? Nearly as tall as a nine-year-old. Impressive."

"I am taller than a nine-year-old!" Amanda realized she had raised her voice, but David just kept smiling. He looked like he was enjoying himself, which only made her more frustrated. "I am a perfectly reasonable height."

"Which is how you got the nickname Mini. That sounds logical."

"I am a perfectly reasonable *petite* height."

David started to say something, but hesitated. He shook his head. The smile still lingered on his face. "I'm just joking, Amanda."

"*Vell*, I don't like your jokes."

They stared at one another for a few beats.

"Hey, Amanda." Benjamin stopped when he reached them. His eyes moved from his sister to David and back to Amanda again. "Everything *oll recht*?"

"Everything is fine," she said through gritted teeth. "He was just leaving."

Recognition flickered in Benjamin's eyes. "Hey, I know who you are. The man who saved Amanda from falling into the goat pen."

"That's not how I would describe him," Amanda muttered, arms still crossed.

Benjamin chuckled. "Now I get it."

"You certain sure do not," Amanda said.

"We heard quite a bit about you that day," Benjamin said.

"Benjamin!" Amanda felt her cheeks flush. "You did not. I never talked about David!"

Benjamin shrugged and smiled. "Agree to disagree."

"I did not!"

"The way I remember it, you were pretty worked up over him."

David gave a smug smile. "Pretty worked up, huh?"

Amanda turned to her brother, eyes flashing. "Benjamin, I will get you back for this. Just wait." She moved her attention to David. "Don't listen to him. He's just trying to make me mad. It's what he does best."

Benjamin put a hand over his heart and gave an exaggerated expression of pain. "Mini Manda, I'm hurt."

Amanda glared at Benjamin.

He winked at her, then looked over to David. "So, what brings you here?"

"No reason," Amanda said before he could answer. "He was just leaving."

The screen door of the front porch swung open and Miriam poked her head out. "Lunch is almost ready." She squinted to get a clearer look at David. "You're the man from the livestock auction, ain't so? The one who rescued Amanda?"

Amanda scowled. "Can everyone stop rewriting history?"

"*Ya*, I am," David shouted across the yard.

"*Vell*, *kumme* join us. Everyone's welcome at our table."

Amanda's teeth hurt from clenching them. Why was everyone on David's side? What was going on?

"He isn't hungry!" Amanda shouted.

"Actually, I've missed lunch at my place," David said. "And it's a mighty long drive back. I wouldn't mind taking you up on that offer."

Miriam nodded. "It'll be ready in about fifteen minutes." She disappeared back into the house with a bang of the screen door.

"I, uh, better go help Miriam," Benjamin said.

"Since when do you run inside to help set the table?" Amanda asked.

Benjamin grinned. "Since I realized I should." He began to stroll away, whistling a tune from the *Ausbund*.

"I'll be right back," Amanda said to David before marching after her brother. "Why are you doing this to me?" she hissed as soon as they were far enough away for David not to hear.

"Doing what?" Benjamin asked with an exaggerated expression of innocence.

Amanda narrowed her eyes. "You know exactly what I mean. Telling David I was talking about him, inviting him to stay for lunch. This is an outrage."

Benjamin paused. Amanda could tell he was searching for the right words. "It'll be *gut* for you."

"Don't patronize me, Benjamin Stoltzfus."

"It'll be fine. Just try and get along over lunch."

"It's almost as if you all have a plan." Amanda inhaled. Her eyes widened. "You *do* have a plan."

Benjamin scratched his jaw. "*Ach, nee.* I mean, not really."

"*Not really* means you absolutely do."

"Well, after David rescued you from the—"

"He did not rescue me," Amanda interrupted.

Benjamin rolled his eyes. "And then you ran into each other at the Feed & Seed and he helped you—"

"How did you know about that?" Amanda interrupted again.

"Billy Tyler mentioned it to Naomi. He thought that David seemed sweet on you."

"He is *not* sweet on me!" Amanda flinched, then lowered her voice. She could only hope that she had not said that loud enough for David to hear. Her emotions were getting the best of her. She was still reeling from the shock of discovering who L.D. really was. And now her family was playing matchmaker? It was just too much. "Why are you meddling?"

Benjamin shifted his weight from one foot to the other. "Um, *vell*, you know…"

"*Nee*, I don't." She enunciated each word with sharp pauses in between, as if speaking to a child. "That's why I'm asking."

Benjamin sighed. "You don't get many suitors, Amanda. We just thought—"

"So I'm a charity case?" Amanda interrupted.

"I didn't say that… Not exactly."

"And you just thought you'd try to throw David and the charity case together?"

"If he showed up here."

"And if he didn't?"

"Naomi and Miriam were thinking of Phase Two. You know, a backup plan, if we needed to track him down." Benjamin grinned. "But he showed up, certain sure. We wanted to place bets, but we didn't, of course. Not the Amish way. But I would have won. Just saying."

"I cannot believe this! All of you whispering about me, making plans… Don't you understand that I don't want to get married?"

"Maybe you just don't want to get married to the wrong guy."

"There is no right guy." An image of L.D. flashed through her mind—or an image of who she had thought he was, anyway. Because he did not exist. Not really.

"Just give him a chance," Benjamin said. "No one's saying you should marry him."

"*Vell*, I should hope not!" Amanda scowled at her brother.

"It's just lunch. And we'll all be there. It's no big deal."

"You're making it into a big deal. It wouldn't have been a big deal if you all had let him leave when he wanted to."

Benjamin's eyes moved beyond Amanda's shoulder, to where David waited awkwardly in the distance, then back to Amanda. "You sure he really wanted to go?"

"*Ya*," Amanda said automatically.

She remembered the look on David's face when she came running out of the farmhouse. It had been disappointment and frustration. She had never felt so humiliated. There was no way he wanted to stay for lunch. Not with her.

But then, a realization swept over her. He had said yes. He could have easily driven by the Old Amish Kitchen and picked up something to go on his way home. So why stay?

She was afraid of the answer. It couldn't be that he was interested in her, could it? Surely, he had just come for farming advice. Any other option made her knees feel weak and her mouth go dry. She told herself that it was irritation. But something deep inside of her whispered otherwise. She was feeling…things.

Well, she would have to stop that. She could not risk her future, especially with a man who had masqueraded as something he was not. David was not the same as L.D. *He* had seemed like an understanding friend, but David could never be that person.

She glanced over at him. He stood with his hands by his sides, waiting patiently. His expression was even and thoughtful. And his face was a little too handsome. This would be easier if he looked like an ogre. Unfortunately, he did not. He looked more like a prince. And that would not do. Because she was not going to fall for a fairy tale romance. Amanda knew those weren't real. Princes did not arrive at your doorstep. Those were just stories. This was real life. She had to protect her dreams, and if she were honest, her pride. She would not give in.

Plus, she was pretty sure that he didn't even like her in that way. Why would he, when no other man had? When he realized that her siblings were trying to set them up, it was going to be utterly humiliating. David was probably already courting a nice Amish woman who couldn't wait to cook his meals and clean his house.

Amanda could never be that girl.

Chapter Five

David should not have accepted an invitation to lunch. What had he been thinking? Amanda did not want him there. And he didn't want to be there, either. Right?

Well, if he admitted it, for just an instant he had thought that maybe they had a connection. They were bantering back and forth, and next thing he knew, Miriam had asked him to stay and it seemed natural to say yes. Or maybe it was his way of getting back at Amanda for her infernal pride. It had certainly riled her up when he'd accepted.

And then there was all that stuff that Benjamin had said. Had Amanda really been talking about him? Could she secretly like him?

No, that was ridiculous. Amanda saw him for exactly who he was: a man who was bound to fail, no matter how hard he tried. She was better than him at farming. At everything, probably. He just wished that he could feel as angry at her as she seemed to be at him.

David watched as she broke away from her conversation with Benjamin and marched over to him. The sun brightened her brown eyes and brought out the highlights in her dark brown hair where it showed beneath her *kapp.* Her cheeks were flushed and she looked pretty. He didn't want to admit it, but she did. David dropped his eyes. Even if he did like her—which he didn't—she would never like him back. Best to push her away before he humiliated himself.

"I didn't expect you to stay for lunch," Amanda said when she reached him. He could not read the masklike expression on her face, but her flat tone communicated plenty.

David adjusted his straw hat. "It's a long drive home. And I didn't want to be impolite. Miriam seemed to want me to stay."

Amanda laughed. David did not expect that. His heart flip-flopped as he watched her eyes light up. He had not seen a genuine smile from her before and it transformed her. "You're right. Miriam doesn't take no for an answer. Maybe you're smarter than you look."

David paused as his mind raced for the best response. Was she making fun of him or just being playful? Or maybe even flirting? No. Surely not. But just in case she was, he needed to respond just right. Not too eager, but not too disinterested, either. He shot her a half smile and said, "So you think I'm smart, huh?"

Amanda raised an eyebrow. "Smarter than you *look.* Which isn't saying much."

David laughed. "Amanda, I don't know what to say to you."

"Then don't say anything," she quipped.

"And let you get the last word? Never."

Amanda stared at him. "*Vell,* I'm waiting."

David racked his brain. This was the time when he needed to show her how clever he was. But he had absolutely nothing witty to say. So he nodded toward the barn instead. "You could show me the goats while we wait for lunch? We still have ten minutes or so."

Amanda hesitated. "I guess we could."

She began to lead him across the farmyard toward the weathered, unpainted barn. A white goose hissed at David and he took a quick sidestep. "You did invite me here to see them," he managed to say once he regained his balance.

"Easy, Belinda," Amanda said to the goose, then glanced over at David and added, "I did not invite you here."

"You suggested that I visit Stoneybrook Farm."

"I suggested that L.D. visit."

"I am L.D., Amanda."

She looked at him as if she were sizing up an Angora's weight and fiber content. "Not so sure about that."

David felt a pain sweep through him. He didn't want to care, but it hurt that Amanda was so disappointed to find out who he really was. Of course, he was just as disappointed about her true identity. But that was different. "You're nothing like M.M., either, you know. She was friendly and fun to talk to." David hadn't meant to say it, but it came out before he could stop himself.

Amanda eyed him as they walked side by side. A beat passed before she said, "So you thought I was fun to talk to."

David had not expected that response. "Uh, I, um, *vell...*"

"So L.D. liked me, anyway." She muttered the words, but David was able to make them out. At least he thought so.

"What was that?" he asked.

"Nothing." She pushed open the barn door with a heavy creak. "Come on."

David wanted to ask what she had meant, if he had heard her correctly. Were her feelings hurt? Did she *want* him to like her? He snuck a sideways glance at her. Her jaw was set and her eyes were fierce. Not likely. Amanda looked like she'd rather court a rattlesnake than him.

He shouldn't have stayed for lunch.

David didn't know what to say as she gave him a tour of the barn, so he stayed silent. Everything was neat and tidy. Amanda kept a good farm, that was for sure. He studied the rows of milking tables and the diesel-powered milking machines. The metal was shiny, wiped clean after the last milking. A few goats bleated in their pens as they followed his movements with curious eyes.

"Most of the goats are up in the west pasture, foraging," Amanda said. "They have shelters up there. We'll rotate them to a different pasture soon. We've got border collies to help with that. The goats in the barn right now are mostly sick or injured. We're keeping a close eye on them."

"I'm surprised you aren't hiding all this from me. I'm a rival, right?"

Amanda's face crumpled for a moment before she smoothed her expression and raised her chin. The look of disappointment had been brief, but David had caught it. "*Vell*, we're still rivals when it comes to getting contracts, but I'm not competing at the fair," she said. "My bishop doesn't approve."

"I'm sorry," he said. The words came out automatically. He had seen how vulnerable she looked in that instant, how lost her expression had seemed.

"It's fine."

"Is it?"

Amanda frowned. She leaned over and reached into the goat pen. A kid with a limp hobbled over to nibble at her fingers. "It's not your problem."

"*Nee*, but that doesn't mean I don't care."

She spun around to face him. "Do you?"

David studied Amanda. Her face was sharp with hard angles, yet soft at the same time. He was beginning to realize that there were more layers to her than he had first thought. But of course there were. She was M.M. too. That made her complicated and fascinating. "Sure." He said the word casually, but it didn't feel casual.

David watched Amanda's throat as she swallowed hard. A few seconds passed. "We should go in to lunch."

"Right." David's face suddenly felt hot. He had said too much. Amanda didn't care about him. She didn't want him to care about her, either. Why had he said that? He needed to pull back from her. "Yep. We've been in here long enough." He turned quickly and headed for the door.

"Yep," Amanda said in a clipped tone.

Hearing that quick agreement made his chest ache. It was obvious that she wasn't interested in him. She didn't have to rub it in. M.M. had seen past his setbacks and insecurities. She had seen that he was worth something. But now, that was over. Amanda saw him for what he really was.

A failure.

Amanda stiffened as they walked into the dining room. Her sisters had replaced the everyday patchwork quilt place mats with crisp, freshly ironed ones, and the room carried the faint pine scent of cleaning fluid. They had been cleaning up, and for David of all people. Why should they work so hard to impress him? What on earth did they see in him?

Maybe the same thing that she had seen in L.D.

Amanda pushed the thought aside. No use in continuing a fantasy that didn't exist. She would stay firmly planted in reality, get this meal over with and never see David Troyer again. A sharp pain formed in her chest at the thought of never writing to L.D. in the future and never receiving another letter. She swallowed hard and slid into her regular seat. Then she frowned when she noticed that the chair beside her, where Naomi always sat, was empty. Every other place was full. Amanda looked over at Naomi, who had taken the extra chair at the end of the table usually reserved for guests, and glared at her. Naomi smiled in response. She knew exactly what she was doing.

David hovered awkwardly beside the empty place setting. "I, uh, guess I'll—"

"*Ya*, you can sit here," Amanda snapped.

David's lips pressed into a tight line.

Amanda had not meant to sound rude. She just felt so frustrated and exposed. "I mean, why don't you sit here?" she said in a gentler tone. "If you want to."

"Sure. *Danki*."

There was shuffling and murmuring throughout the room as the large extended family settled down for the meal. David stared at his plate and waited. He shifted in his seat. Amanda wondered how she could act normally when it was so obvious that he didn't want to be there.

"Let's pray," Miriam said. The noise died abruptly

as everyone stopped their conversations to pray silently. Amanda tried to keep her eyes closed, but she couldn't resist opening one eye and sneaking a sidelong glance at David. His brow was furrowed, his jaw tight. Amanda tried to pay attention to her prayer, but found herself staring at him. Then his eyes opened and he made direct eye contact with her. She jumped in her seat—imperceptibly she hoped—and squeezed her eyes shut. He had caught her watching him. And when she should have been praying, of all times!

Of course, he had snuck a peek at her too. Even so, her cheeks still burned and she knew her face was flushed with embarrassment. At least no one else had seen. What had she been thinking? And what had *he* been thinking?

Miriam cleared her throat to signal the end of the prayer, and the dining room erupted in noise. Dishes clanged as they were passed around, Benjamin spoke loudly across the table to Naomi and they both laughed, Abby fussed in John's arms, Emma slathered a slice of sourdough bread with butter while Caleb napped in a playpen in the corner of the room, and Miriam and Leah spoke in low voices, heads close together. Amanda was sure she knew what they were talking about and she glared at them when their eyes met hers. They both smiled sweetly and scooped out big servings of green-bean casserole before passing the bowl to Emma. Outside, a bird sang in the big oak tree as the wind rustled through the leaves. Caleb shifted in his sleep and sucked on his pacifier, but his eyes stayed closed.

David sat in silence, his attention on his plate. Amanda knew she should say something to him. He looked out of place and alone. She had no idea what the right thing to say would be, but she had to try. She would show everyone that she was the bigger person. "So what did you think of my goat barn?" Amanda asked.

"*Our* goat barn," Benjamin said without missing a beat. "I've mucked it out often enough."

Amanda sighed. Why did everything have to be so difficult? Being nice was harder than it seemed. "Fine. *Our* goat barn," she repeated with a little too much emphasis on the word.

"Amanda likes to think that she owns the place," Benjamin said before Amanda could get another word in. "But Miriam's really the one who runs the show." He nodded toward Miriam as he stuffed a big bite of sourdough bread into his mouth.

Miriam rolled her eyes but did not deny it.

David's eyes moved from one sibling to the other, but he did not respond. Amanda felt a stab of sympathy. Outsiders couldn't always understand her family's dynamics. "They're joking," she said.

Benjamin chewed quickly and swallowed hard. "No, I'm not."

Naomi grinned. "Is the truth a joke?"

Amanda scowled at Naomi. "That is not the truth. Well, the part about Miriam being bossy is. But I don't go around like I own the place."

Miriam choked on her ice water, coughed and set the glass down. "You don't go around—"

"*Nee*, I do not," Amanda interrupted.

Miriam raised an eyebrow.

Benjamin chuckled.

Why did her siblings have to poke fun at her while David was here? They were the worst matchmakers ever.

"I put a lot of work into this farm," Amanda said, more forcefully than she meant to. "Is that a crime?"

The room fell silent and everyone's attention swung to Amanda. She realized that she had spoken too harshly. Her response had been inappropriate. Like it or not, *they* were joking. But she was not. This was too personal to joke about. Her cheeks heated—for the second time in five minutes—and she looked down. She could hear the clock ticking on the wall and the distant bleat of a goat in the farmyard.

"*Vell*, all that work has paid off," David said. He glanced over at Amanda quickly, then dropped his eyes. "It's a well-run farm. I'm impressed."

Amanda felt a strange burst of gratitude. David had stood up for her and saved her from embarrassment. The silence ended, Amanda's outburst forgotten, and the table fell back into low murmurs and clattering silverware.

"*Danki*," Amanda said quietly.

"It's true." David shifted in his seat. "And I, uh, appreciated the tour."

"You did?"

"Of course."

Amanda's heart warmed a little. Maybe David wasn't quite so bad, after all. "So, you think I'm *gut* at my job?"

"Of course I do. Haven't I been writing to you for advice for months?"

Amanda cringed. She lowered her voice to a whisper and leaned closer. "*Ya*, but they don't know."

David's brow crinkled. "But why wouldn't you tell…" Then realization flickered across his face and he cleared his throat, then looked away.

Amanda wanted to sink under the table. She had to

fix this, and fast. David could not think that she had been sweet on L.D. "I'm just careful not to overshare. You can see how my siblings are."

David smiled and glanced back at her. "I'm getting the picture."

Their eyes locked and Amanda got the strange sensation that they understood each other. For the first time, she was looking at L.D., not David. Her stomach fluttered and her mouth felt dry. She had to look away. When she did, Amanda saw that Benjamin had stopped eating and was staring at them. The butterflies in her belly turned into a sharp jolt.

"Wait. You two already knew each other?" He set down his fork and folded his arms as he leaned forward.

Amanda's eyes widened.

Leah's and Naomi's side conversation stopped abruptly and Leah's head whipped around. "You knew each other before the auction?"

"How?" Naomi asked as her eyes narrowed. "You hardly ever leave the farm except to go to church meetings or the Feed & Seed."

Amanda didn't answer. Instead, she glanced at David, then to the rest of the faces staring at her around the table. Emma's brow furrowed. John bounced Abby in his lap as he exchanged a quick look with Leah. Miriam dropped her napkin on her plate and leaned back in her chair. "Sounds like you've got a story to tell," she said.

"*Nee.*" Amanda shook her head. "No story."

David studied Amanda's face for an instant, then said, "It's not a very *gut* story." He shrugged, his expression bland. Amanda could tell that he was trying to look detached. Was it because he was hiding his feelings for M.M., or because he did not have any? "I started a goat farm, saw a flyer from another goat farmer on the bulletin board at a feedstore and wrote for advice." He shrugged. "That farmer happened to be Amanda. That's it."

"That's it?" Naomi asked. She did not look convinced.

"So you've been writing each other in secret ever since?" Benjamin asked. He grinned. "I didn't know you had it in you, Amanda. A secret courtship!"

"*Nee!*" Amanda shouted. She frowned and tried again, quieter this time. "I mean *nee*, we weren't courting. It was business. Just business."

David nodded. "Strictly business."

Amanda crumpled a little bit inside, but was sure not to show it. She wanted to convince everyone that there had been nothing between them, but she didn't want David to agree. Was he taking her lead, or was he telling the truth? Even if she wasn't interested in him now, she didn't want him to reject her. That would prove that she wasn't courtship material to anybody—not even her secret pen pal.

"So, this meeting that you two planned in secret—" Emma began to ask, before Amanda cut her off.

"We didn't plan it in secret."

"She invited me," David said.

"*Vell*, that's not… I mean…it didn't happen quite like that."

David breathed in and out. "I just meant that we weren't keeping anything from anyone."

"*Recht*," Amanda said. "Because I didn't invite you."

"You were always a terrible liar, Amanda," Benjamin said.

"I am *not* lying!"

David smoothed out his napkin. He did not look at the people around him.

"She only suggested I visit a *gut* goat farm. She didn't invite me to meet her. I didn't mean…"

"See!" Amanda said. "I'm not lying."

"Uh-huh. You two have been secretly exchanging letters and then he shows up here." Benjamin raised his eyebrows. "But you're being completely honest with us."

"It's none of your business anyway, Benjamin Stoltzfus!"

Benjamin raised his hands in mock appeasement, but he was grinning. "*Oll recht, oll recht.* It was an innocent coincidence for your secret pen pal to show up here. Got it."

David rubbed his fingers along his chin. "Uh, it was, actually. I mean, I didn't know I was writing to Amanda, so it was all just a big misunderstanding, I guess. It was all a mistake."

"She didn't tell you who she was?" Miriam asked. A flicker of interest passed over her features. Amanda narrowed her eyes. Miriam might act like she was the only mature adult in the family, but she enjoyed a good story from the Amish telegraph, same as anyone.

"It wasn't relevant," Amanda said.

"Wait," Emma said. "So when he saved you from falling into the goat pen at the auction, you didn't know that he was your pen pal?"

"Okay, first of all, he did not save me—"

Amanda was interrupted by a chorus of groans.

David gave a smile that looked closer to a smirk. "Now, that's where we're going to have to disagree."

"I thought you were on my side!" Amanda hissed.

"I'm on the side of truth."

"Truth," Amanda muttered and rolled her eyes. "You're playing fast and loose with it, if you ask me."

"*I'm* playing fast and loose with the truth?"

They stared at one another for a few beats.

"Children, children," Benjamin said. He was grinning. The entire family was enjoying this way too much. "You're getting off subject."

Amanda rolled her eyes again. "*Nee*, we did not know who the other one was on the day he did not rescue me."

Benjamin chuckled. "Interesting."

"Amanda's been a lot of help, actually," David said.

Amanda swung her attention back to him. How could he go from criticizing her to defending her so quickly? Maybe he had just been teasing. L.D. had seemed pretty serious. But David was much more mischievous. If she could call it that. Another word for it would be *annoying*. The least he could do was admit that she had not needed rescuing that day.

"She's really *gut* at what she does," David continued.

Amanda's thoughts cut off abruptly. Was he complimenting her? Was he telling everyone that he recognized her value, when no other man had? Amanda's chest swelled with warmth. She almost forgot that he had been teasing her. Almost.

"Better than anyone else I know who raises livestock," David added.

Amanda forgot the teasing completely.

"You really think so?" she asked quietly. Her heart thumped so loudly she wondered if he could hear it. She wanted to leap up, hug him and shout for joy. It was very hard to sit still and act nonchalant.

"Sure, I do. Why do you think I kept asking you for advice? You gave me the information that I needed to get my farm off to a *gut* start," David said.

The warmth faded. Was the relationship really all business to him? Of course it was. Why else would he have kept writing? She had deceived herself into thinking that he had enjoyed their exchange on a personal level.

"And now I've got a chance to compete at the livestock show." David's expression shifted as soon as he said the words. His eyes cut to Amanda's. "Sorry you can't go too."

"I can go. I just can't compete."

"Oh." David's forehead crinkled. "So, you're okay with that?"

"Of course I am." She forced out the words, and hoped that it was not a lie, since she *wanted* to be okay with it.

"*Gut.*" He nodded but the frown stayed on his face. "That's *gut.* I thought…"

Amanda ignored the stab inside her chest and waved him away. "It's fine. I'll go and see the livestock."

"You didn't tell us you weren't entering the show," Miriam said.

"Bishop Amos said no."

Miriam sighed. "I'm sorry, Amanda. I knew it meant a lot to you."

Amanda shook her head. "*Nee.* It's not a big deal." She was not going to admit to everyone that her heart was broken. She shouldn't care this much about competing. That was not the Amish way. She stared at her water glass and willed the tears not to form.

"*Gut*," Benjamin said. "I was afraid you'd be crushed." His smile reached his eyes. Her brother's genuine relief only made Amanda feel worse. No one could understand how much this meant to her. They would only think that she was seeking vainglory. Benjamin was always sensitive and understanding beneath his fun-loving teasing, but she would not even admit the full truth to him. Better to let them all think that she was better at being Amish than she actually was. She knew she didn't fit inside the neat little box that a lot of other Amish women did. She had hoped that if she could show everyone how good she was at farmwork, they would accept her for who she was, even though she was different. Now, she had lost that chance. But if she explained all of that, she would have to admit that she did not belong.

"Nope," Amanda said. "I'm not crushed. Not at all." She knew that wasn't really true. Not yet, anyway. But she was trying. Maybe, if she kept trying, she could let go of that need for validation.

"Then this works out great," Benjamin said. He leaned forward as his eyes flashed the way they always did when he got excited. "You can help David win, since you won't be competing against him."

"Oh." Amanda's mouth opened to say more but nothing came out.

David frowned. "I'm not sure…" He adjusted one of his black suspenders. "I mean… *Vell*, I don't think Amanda should go to any trouble for me."

Amanda tilted her chin upward. "It's no trouble." She wasn't sure how the words fell out of her mouth. Maybe she wanted to show off a little by telling him how much she knew. Or maybe she wanted to…help?

David's frown morphed into a quick smile. "Really?"

"No trouble at all."

"I thought you might…" David shrugged. "We were pretty competitive not too long ago. No hard feelings?"

"Of course not." And then Amanda whispered a quick prayer for forgiveness under her breath. Because that was definitely a lie. She was jealous that David was getting to do what she could not. And now, helping him win was only going to make it sting worse. She should not have agreed to help him. Her mind grasped for a way to backtrack. "Although it might not be the best idea since—"

"*Ach*, it's a great idea," Benjamin interrupted.

"I'm not sure there's much I actually can do to help," Amanda said.

"The greatest goat farmer of all time doesn't have any advice?" Naomi asked.

"Okay, that's just unnecessary," Amanda said.

"You're right," Naomi said. "Sorry. But you *are* a know-it-all when it comes to goats."

Amanda heaved a heavy sigh. "*Oll recht.* Fine. But only when it comes to goats."

Naomi nodded. "Fair."

"And only because I do know it all when it comes to goats," Amanda muttered under her breath.

"I heard that," Naomi said.

Miriam pushed back her chair and stood up. "We'll take care of the kitchen. Amanda, why don't you go out and show David more of the farm? You can catch him up on all the latest techniques that you've been reading about and putting into practice here. That's a *gut* way to help him."

Amanda's jaw tightened. What had she gotten herself

into? Could she stop thinking of David as a rival and help him succeed where she could not? A good Plain person would. But Amanda wasn't sure that she was quite good enough for that. Instead, all she could think about was that David was getting to do what she wanted, while she was shut out from it. And now she had to play nice, after he had made it clear that all he had ever wanted from her was business advice?

L.D. had never existed and never would. Amanda had to accept that, no matter how much it hurt.

Chapter Six

David was reeling with suppressed emotion. He had tried so hard not to show what he was feeling at the dinner table. Did anyone suspect that he had fallen for M.M.? Surely not. He had done a good job downplaying their pen pal relationship as soon as he picked up on the fact that Amanda wanted to hide it from her siblings. The question was why. Could it be because she was embarrassed to admit that they had fallen for one another without ever meeting? It did sound pretty silly. And Amanda's family would definitely give her a hard time about it. They were loving but also rowdy and not for the faint of heart. David could tell that teasing was their way to show closeness, but he suspected it could go too far sometimes. Families had a way of doing that, even when they meant well.

Then again, there was the more obvious possibility. Amanda might not have ever fallen for L.D. The feelings might have only been one way. David knew that *he* had been smitten, but maybe he had misread Amanda's intentions in her letters. After all, M.M. had stressed their friendship throughout their correspondence. She'd never said anything more.

But she had invited him to Stoneybrook Farm so they could meet. That did seem like evidence that she had been sweeter on L.D. than she wanted to admit. Of course, she didn't like what she saw when he actually arrived as David. Whatever he had been able to pull off on paper, he had failed at in person. Maybe he just wasn't good-looking enough for her. Or maybe he had teased her too much, just like her family had at the dinner table. For all her toughness, David was beginning to realize that Amanda was soft on the inside, although she would never admit it.

He wondered how to put all those thoughts into words as Amanda led him down the hallway. The old wooden floorboards creaked under their weight. "I, uh, appreciate the tour," he said as she pushed open the screen door and they stepped out into the bright sunlight. He pulled down the brim of his straw hat to block the glare.

"Like I said, it's no problem." She strode forward, back straight, eyes ahead, as if he weren't there. The big Anatolian shepherd lifted his head when Amanda reached the last porch step. "Come on, Ollie," she said and the dog leaped up, tail wagging. He circled them both, then lowered his nose to the ground and sniffed an invisible trail that led toward the pastureland. Amanda did not slow down. "We can go up and check on the goats in the west field," she said, eyes still focused ahead.

"Sure," David said. "That sounds *gut. Danki* for showing me around."

"I need to go up there anyway."

"*Recht.* Okay." David rubbed the back of his neck. It was hard not to take her cool demeanor personally. This was not at all how she had seemed in her letters. Was he really that unlikable in person?

They didn't speak as she led him up the long, sloping hill. Tall grass rippled in the breeze, like waves in a green sea. Wildflowers lay scattered across the pasture, the white petals glowing beneath the sun as it warmed the earth. He could hear the distant chime of bells and see the goats in a faraway field. They were small at that distance, no bigger than toys. Soon, David began to feel winded and lagged behind. Amanda forged on, head up, elbows pumping, until she finally noticed that he was no longer beside her. She glanced behind her and sighed. "What are you doing back there?"

"Just catching my breath." David's calves burned along with his chest. "It's a steep hill."

"Not really."

David swept his hand in front of him. "This is steep. I can see that it's steep."

Amanda shrugged. "Doesn't seem like it to me."

"My farm is pretty flat. And small. I'm not used to all this hiking."

Amanda sighed and jogged down the hill to stand beside him. She was not even short of breath. Ollie bounded behind her and barked when she didn't keep walking. Amanda gave him a quick pat on the head, then put her hands on her hips and looked past David as a smile lit up her face. He wondered what she saw and turned to follow her gaze. He only saw more of the same land.

"It's beautiful, isn't it?" Her eyes took on a dreamy quality, hazy and happy.

David stared down the hill, in the direction that they had come. He saw the sloping green pastureland crisscrossed with white fences and patches of tall weeds. The farmhouse sat two-thirds of the way down the hill, and looked quaint and homey. The long hillside continued past the house, into the neighboring property, until it leveled out into an orchard. The rows of peach and pear trees seemed neat and orderly against the haphazard fences and patchwork of pastures on the Stoltzfus property. Beyond the rows of fruit trees, a pond lay nestled in the valley, its water flashing in the bright midday light and reflecting the blue sky. Above it all, hawks rode the warm air currents, circling the pastures, fields and orchards on silent wings, their shadows racing over the ground when they passed in front of the sun.

It looked like much of the farmland in Lancaster County. Scenic and peaceful, but not unique. But David realized that to Amanda it *was* unique. This was her farm, her dream. He began to see the land through her eyes. "It is beautiful," he whispered.

Amanda moved her gaze to his and smiled. "You see it, don't you?"

"I think I do." And the realization warmed his heart and made him feel closer to Amanda. She seemed like M.M. again, starry-eyed with her love for the land her family owned. They stayed like that for a long moment, not speaking, just appreciating the view together, and David wished that moment could last forever.

But it had to be broken. Ollie came bounding toward them, barked and circled Amanda. "*Oll recht*," she said as she turned her attention away from the scenery. "We're coming."

The rest of the hike felt friendlier, and when they reached a creek, Amanda showed him where to ford it, instead of leaving him to figure it out on his own. "This is the best spot," she said as she hopped onto a large, flat stone.

"Don't slip," he said as he followed her, then lost his balance as soon as he landed. He threw out his arms to steady himself and Amanda grabbed his wrist as he teetered on the edge of the stone.

"I won't," Amanda said in a deadpan tone. "But maybe you should take your own advice."

David thought she was making fun of him until he looked over and saw that she was smiling. "Fair enough."

They both laughed.

"Hey, is this how the farm gets its name?" David asked after he cleared the last stone and landed with a soft thump on the grassy bank.

Amanda looked at him. "No one's ever asked me that before. Usually, I have to point it out to people."

"Seems pretty obvious." He waved his hand. "Stones. A brook."

"You'd think."

"Did you name it?" he asked as he fell into place beside her and they continued up the hill.

She took a deep breath and let it out slowly. Her expression shifted. "*Nee*, my parents did."

"Oh." M.M. had mentioned that she and her siblings had inherited the farm after their parents passed away. He wondered what he should say. He didn't want to bring up painful memories, but he sensed she needed to talk about it. "Did you get your love of farming from them?"

"*Ya*, they loved this place. It was so important to them. Miriam was old enough to take over when they died. She gave up a lot to take care of us and make sure we didn't lose it. Then, as we got older, we all learned how to run it alongside her. But none of them love it like I do. I think I'm like my parents in that way." She paused and David turned his head to study her face as they continued walking up the hill. Sunlight highlighted her brown eyelashes, turning them golden. But even in the warm light, her eyes looked sad and full of need. "It makes me feel closer to them," she finally added in a quiet voice. "And I hope they'd be proud of me, if they could see me today."

David swallowed hard. So much about Amanda suddenly made sense now. She wanted so badly to live up to the memory of the people she admired most. She wanted to stay connected to them in the only way she knew how. As he stared at her, all he could think was how much he wanted to reach out and touch the soft plane of her cheek and tell her that he understood and appreciated her. He wanted her to know that he saw her. "I'm sure they would be," he said instead.

She stopped walking and swung her attention to him. "You really think so?"

"Of course I do."

She held his gaze for a long, intense moment, before turning back toward their destination and plodding onward.

Amanda watched David as he interacted with her goats. He crouched down, scratched under their chins and patted their flanks. He studied their coats and nodded. "You've got a *gut* herd."

"Of course I do."

David looked up and Amanda grinned at him.

He grinned back. "And you've got plenty of pride too, ain't so?"

"I like to call it confidence."

David raised an eyebrow. "Is that what they're calling it these days?"

"Yep."

He shook his head as he raised himself off his knee, but he was still smiling. "So we're going to move them to the next pasture?"

"*Ya.* They've foraged all they can in this one. We'll keep rotating them until they eventually *kumme* back to this pasture." She gave a loud, piercing whistle without warning, and David jumped.

Amanda chuckled. "Sorry, didn't mean to startle you. Just need to get the boys down here."

"The boys?"

"Chocolate, Chip!" she shouted instead of answering him. "Let's go!"

Two black-and-white border collies appeared from behind the herd and came bounding down the hill. They hurtled to a stop at Amanda's feet, tails wagging low to the ground, ears pricked and ready.

"Come by!" she shouted and the two dogs took off, ears back, mud flying from beneath their paws. They circled the herd and crouched low to the ground, inching forward and forcing the goats toward the left. Amanda exhaled and smiled. These were the moments she loved in life. She felt so free, up here at the top of the hill, watching her dogs move together in a silent dance alongside the goats.

"I've never seen border collies in action before," David said.

"It's not so common to use them with goats," Amanda said. "But it works well."

"It certain sure does." David adjusted the brim of his straw hat to shield his eyes from the sun as he followed the dogs' carefully orchestrated movements. "I'm impressed."

Amanda cut him a sharp glance. "You are?" She thought she caught a flicker of insecurity in his expression, but that didn't seem like him.

"Of course I am." He swept his arm across the pasture. "With all of it. My farm's nothing like this."

"We've been doing this for three generations. It takes time."

David nodded, eyes still on the dogs. A nanny broke loose and trotted in the opposite direction. Chip darted behind the female goat while Chocolate continued to push the rest of the herd to the left side of the field. "To me!" Amanda shouted and the dogs yipped, then shifted the direction of the herd toward her. "This way," she said to David and opened a gate behind them. They strode out together and the herd followed as Chocolate and Chip pushed them through. A few stragglers missed the entrance, but Chip darted back and rounded them up. His ears stayed flat against his head, his eyes sharp with concentration, but his mouth was open in what looked like a grin. "I always think they're smiling," Amanda said.

"The goats?" David asked.

She laughed. "*Nee*, the dogs."

David chuckled. "*Ya*, you're right."

"They're happiest when they're working," Amanda said.

David hesitated, then said, "Like you."

Amanda smiled softly. "Like me." Amanda wanted to acknowledge what David had said because it seemed like he understood her. But she was afraid to admit it. She thought about it as they traipsed across a grassy field, trampling tall weeds underfoot, while the dogs herded the goats behind them. "You sound like L.D.," Amanda finally said.

David's eyes flicked to hers. "That's because I am," he said gently.

"Are you?"

"Of course."

Amanda gazed deeply into his eyes. "So, you were being the real you on paper, not in person?"

"Didn't you just say I sound like the version of me that was on paper, right here, in person?"

"Humph."

David chuckled. "Is it that irritating for me to have a *gut* point?"

"*Ya*. It certain sure is."

David's chuckle turned into a full-blown laugh.

"Am I that funny to you?"

"When you say things like that."

"I don't know whether to be mad at you or laugh with you."

"Maybe try laughing."

"Maybe."

The goat bells clanged as the herd trotted across the field. "Away to me!" Amanda shouted. The dogs turned on their heels, splattering mud, and shot around to the left of the herd to begin pushing them toward the right, where a fence cut between pastures. When they reached it, Amanda unlatched a gate and shouted, "To me!" The dogs herded the goats from behind, forcing them through the gate and into a fresh pasture.

Amanda latched the gate behind them and gave a satisfied sigh. She whistled and the dogs lurched away from the herd to come running. They approached so quickly that they had to skid to a stop, tearing up the damp earth with their paws. Amanda smiled and knelt down to scratch behind their ears. "*Gut* boys," she murmured. "*Gut* job."

"It's really something to see you at work," David said.

Amanda stood up and brushed her hands on her apron. "You think so?"

"I do."

"You said I wasn't a serious farmer, remember?"

David rolled his eyes. "Let's move past that. As I recall, you said some things you might regret too."

Amanda flashed a mischievous grin. "So you regret saying that?"

"*Ach*, you know I do. Look at you."

Amanda's grin slipped into a smug smile.

"But if you keep that look on your face, I might take it back."

"What look?" Amanda asked in a tone of exaggerated innocence.

David raised an eyebrow. "You know exactly what I mean."

Amanda laughed. "Maybe I do."

The sun was slipping down and the light looked softer toward the horizon, at the bottom of the long hill. Far in the distance, the pond sparkled beneath the long, afternoon rays, and shadows stretched out from the isolated oak trees that dotted the pastureland. "We should head back," Amanda said. "It's getting late." But she had another reason for wanting to leave. The conversation was making her feel warm and mushy inside, the same way that L.D.'s letters had. That was not the way that David was supposed to make her feel.

"Thanks for the tour," David said as they began to head down the hill. Ollie started to follow but Amanda stopped him. "Stay here, *bu*. Guard the herd." Ollie gazed at her with big brown eyes, then turned and loped back toward the goats.

"Tell me about your place," Amanda said as they headed down toward the faraway farmhouse.

David's expression shifted and he looked away. "*Ach*, my farm is a lot smaller than yours. Not much to tell, really."

"Where is it?"

"The Little Creek church district, two miles off the main highway down Sugar Maple Lane, right past the Byler pear orchard."

Amanda had never been out there, but she had heard of the Bylers' orchard. "I'd like to see it."

David rubbed the back of his neck. "*Ya*. But there's not much to see."

Amanda cut him a sidelong glance. Was he discouraging her from visiting? Now, when things finally seemed to be going well between them? "You don't want me to visit?"

"I didn't say that."

"You may as well have."

David took off his straw hat, ran his fingers through his hair and slammed it back onto his head. "Not everything has to be a fight, Amanda."

"I didn't make it into one."

They both grunted. Amanda snuck a look at David and he snuck a look at her. She almost smiled because they had both done the same thing at the same time. Maybe they weren't so disconnected, after all.

David didn't quite smile, but his eyes softened. "You know, I really am sorry you can't compete at the show. I know it's got to be a letdown."

Was this a peace offering? Amanda hoped it was, so she allowed herself to open up a little, even though the tightening in her chest warned against it. "*Ya*, I don't understand why you're allowed to compete and I'm not. My bishop didn't even hesitate. He said it wasn't the Amish way."

David rubbed his hand along his jaw. "I don't know. My church district is just a little looser about things like that, I guess. I wasn't even planning on competing—"

"What do you mean, you weren't planning on competing?" Amanda interrupted.

David shrugged. "I wasn't really interested. But then I realized that it could be *gut* for business. I need a big contract to really get the farm off the ground."

Amanda stopped walking. David kept on for a few steps before he realized, stopped and turned around. "What's the matter?"

Amanda's brow creased. "You get to compete and you don't even care?" This had been her big chance to prove herself. And now *he* got to go and it didn't even matter to him.

"I didn't say I didn't care. I just hadn't thought of competing. It's not something I like to do."

"*Vell*, you've been competitive toward me, certain sure."

"That's different."

"Is it?" She stared at him for a few beats, but he didn't respond. "Competing in that show meant a lot to me. It isn't fair that you get to do it when it means nothing to you."

"I don't think you get it." David frowned as he kept his eyes on the hillside ahead of them. "It'll mean an awful lot if I get a contract."

"I don't think you get it, either. It would mean an awful lot if…" Amanda cut herself off. She wanted to tell him how much she had to prove, but that would be too embarrassing.

"If what?"

"Nothing. Forget it." The words came out sharper than she meant.

"Fine."

"Fine." Amanda pressed her lips together and kept walking. They went the rest of the way down the hill in silence as she replayed the conversation in her head. It wasn't David's fault that he got to compete when she didn't. She should apologize. The thought made her toes curl with indignation, but she would manage. Somehow.

David cut directly to his buggy horse when they reached the farmyard. The black mare snorted and shook her mane when he began to untie the lead from the hitching post. "Look," Amanda said. "It isn't your fault that you don't care about the competition." David raised his eyebrows, then led the horse to the buggy and began to hitch her up. She whinnied and chomped at the bit as he worked.

"You're not going to say anything?"

"I don't know what to say to that."

"I'm telling you that it's okay."

"*Vell, danki* for giving me permission to have my feelings."

Amanda squeezed her eyes shut. This was not going how she had planned. She opened her eyes and took a deep breath. "I'm trying to apologize."

David finally looked up from the harness. "Are you?"

"*Ya.* I just said so, didn't I? But maybe it wasn't the best attempt."

David stared at her. She hadn't noticed how deep and clear his eyes were until now, highlighted by the low sun as it filtered through the tree line and bathed the farmyard in yellow. There was depth there that she had not been willing to see before.

But why was she thinking of his eyes? They were in the middle of a spat. No, a lively discussion would be a better way of explaining it. She didn't want to fight him. She just wanted him to understand her. But wanting that could only lead to attachment, which could only lead to her throwing herself at him, getting her heart broken or ending up a farmer's wife without a farm of her own. Amanda frowned. *Wife?* How could she let her thoughts run away like this? It was preposterous. He didn't even want her to visit his farm.

"That's something we can agree on," David said.

"*Vell,* at least I tried."

"Debatable."

"You could try too, you know."

"You think I'm not trying?"

Judging by his expression, Amanda had touched on

something raw and she wished she could take it back. "I don't know."

He looked back down to buckle a harness. Metal jangled and the leather creaked. "You were saying something about apologizing?" He glanced back up at her with what might have been a smug expression, or maybe just a playful one. She couldn't tell if he was trying to make peace or push her buttons.

Amanda's jaw clenched. She forced herself to relax. She could do this. She could be the bigger person. "I was frustrated because you get to compete in the show even though you don't care about it. That wasn't fair of me." The truth was she was more than frustrated—she was jealous. But good Amish folk weren't supposed to be jealous, so how could she admit it?

"I do care," David said. "I care a lot."

"You said you didn't."

David exhaled through his teeth as he latched the last buckle. "I care about the bigger picture. This is about a lot more than a competition for me."

Amanda stared at him. She could feel the frustration rising again and she clenched her fists to keep it in check. "It's about a lot more than that for me too. Can't you see that?"

David patted the horse on the neck, then walked to the driver's side of the buggy. "You make it pretty hard to see it," he said before he hopped in.

Amanda shook her head. "You acted like you knew me in your letters. But you don't. You don't understand anything about me."

"And you don't understand anything about me," David said softly. "But I'm sorry too. I'm sorry you're hurting and I'm sorry I made you feel like you aren't welcome at my farm. You are. And I'm… I'm sorry I came here today. Seems like I've only made things worse." He snapped the reins and turned his attention straight ahead. "Walk on," he said. And then he was gone in a trail of dust, a scattering of chickens and a hiss from Belinda the guard goose, who ran across the farmyard, wings flapping, to chase the buggy until it cleared the gate.

"*Vell*, where have you been, Belinda?" Amanda threw up her hands. "You should have chased him away as soon as he got here. That would have saved me some heartache and confusion. Because I'm not sure what to feel right now."

Belinda stared at Amanda with her beady black eyes, then ruffled her feathers and waddled past her.

"Alone. As always," Amanda muttered. Why couldn't she communicate better with David? Why couldn't they just get along?

Because his opinion mattered, that was why. And she was too afraid to hear what he really thought of her. She had already given her heart to L.D. What if she wasn't good enough for him now that they had met in person? That would mean that she was truly unwanted, with no hope of ever being seen and appreciated for who she really was.

With stakes that high, of course it pushed her over the edge every time she saw him.

And the timing could not be worse. The competition was tomorrow. Could she overcome the hurt and jealousy in order to show up and support David? She had said she would. And, deep down, she wanted to. Why was this competition so important to her, really? It wasn't about business. Sure, that was important, but what she really wanted was for everyone, and most especially David, to see her worth. Maybe it was time to feel confident in herself regardless of whether she had anyone else's approval. Ha! Easier said than done.

But she had to try. Otherwise, she would never find peace. She would do her best to let it go. Even if it killed her. Which, in that moment, it felt like it just might.

Chapter Seven

David lay awake that night, staring at the black sky outside his bedroom window. An owl hooted and a dog barked somewhere in the distance, but there was no moon and he could only see darkness. He sighed, punched down his feather pillow and tried to get comfortable. Tomorrow was the competition and he could not stop thinking about Amanda's words from earlier that day. She did not think that he was trying. She did not think that he had anything to lose. After all their letters, she still could not understand how much was on the line for him.

David rolled over and squeezed his eyes shut, trying to force himself to sleep. But the thoughts kept churning through his head. The truth was, he had never fully admitted the truth to M.M. He had been too ashamed to let her know how close he was to failing and losing the farm. Sure, he had hinted some, and he had certainly asked for advice, but he had not come right out and said it. Was it possible that Amanda didn't realize how much was at stake for him? Did she really think that all this came easily to him?

Could she actually be jealous? He pushed aside the

silly thought and laughed out loud. The sound of his voice broke into the silence of the dark bedroom. Amanda, jealous of *him*? She had the biggest and best goat farm in the county. And she knew exactly what she was doing. David, on the other hand, felt like he was stumbling through his days, trying his best, but making too many mistakes along the way. If he were honest, he was the one who was jealous of her.

There, he had admitted it. He was jealous of Amanda. She had it all—a big, prosperous farm and a natural talent for running it. While he, on the other hand, seemed to make a mess of everything. David sighed and punched down his pillow again. He was Amish. He shouldn't be jealous. He should be happy for Amanda—and he was. He just wished that he could be as good at everything as she was. "Help me to appreciate the talents You've given me, *Gott*, even though I'm not as successful as Amanda," he whispered. "And help me to trust You with the future. It seems like I just make things worse, no matter how hard I try. And not just with my farm—I think I've messed things up with Amanda too. I couldn't tell her how I feel, how insecure she makes me, when I should have. If there's a way to fix that, please help me to do it."

The next thing that David knew, the sun was pouring through his window directly into his eyes and the birds were chirping. For an instant, he struggled to pull himself out of the warm, deep pool of sleep. A vague memory tugged at his mind. There was something he had to do today.

David bolted upright. The competition. He threw off the covers and jumped into his Sunday best quicker than he ever had. He splashed water onto his face from the basin, combed his hair and sprinted out the door. Today was the day that might decide his future.

When David arrived at the fairgrounds, his first thought was that he wished M.M. were there. His family would come later, in time for the competition, after they finished the farm chores. So for now, he had to plunge into the noisy crowd, alone. Cows bellowed, goats bleated and horses whinnied. An enormous Clydesdale plodded alongside him, and David sidestepped just in time to avoid one of the giant hooves. "Sorry about that," a man wearing a cowboy hat and flannel shirt said. "Didn't see you there." *Right*, David thought, *that's the problem*. No one saw him. Or at least that was the way it felt. Was there anyone who really understood him and his struggles? M.M. had. But Amanda? She definitely did not.

The smell of fried dough and buttered popcorn wafted toward him, mingling with the heavy scent of earth and animals. People shouted and competitors strode past him, looking as if they knew exactly what they were doing. He had to ask directions twice before he found the right ring. The competition looked mighty fierce. He reminded himself that it was okay if he didn't win. There might be other chances to catch the eye of a company ready to offer a big contract. But he knew that wasn't true. He had just gone over the books again last night. Time was definitely running out. He glanced around the ring. There were no familiar faces. He hoped his family would arrive soon, but he knew there would be plenty of distractions before they reached him. His little sister would want to stop and see everything as they made their way through the fairgrounds.

David had just unloaded the last of his goats from the

hired trailer and waved goodbye to the *Englisch* driver when he heard a familiar voice. The sound sent a wave of relief through him, even though he didn't think it should.

"I didn't expect to see you here," he said as he turned around to face Amanda. She looked hesitant, even though her shoulders were squared and she stood straight as she stared up at him.

"I told you I'd *kumme* even though I can't compete."

"*Ya*, but I wasn't sure you'd *kumme* over here to see me." David rubbed the back of his neck. He wanted to tell her that he was glad to see her, but was afraid to admit it. He needed to focus on winning the show. Exposing his vulnerabilities would distract him when he needed to be his sharpest.

Amanda paused before speaking. "This arena is where all the goats are," Amanda said after a moment, without making eye contact. "Of course I had to *kumme* over here."

"*Recht*. Of course." David tried to ignore the little drop in his stomach. "But it must be hard for you to be here when you can't compete. I know how important that was to you." David held his breath. He wanted her to understand that he cared, without having to say it.

David thought he saw a flicker of emotion behind Amanda's eyes, before her expression hardened. She brushed a fleck of dirt from her apron. "It's fine. I'm fine."

She said the words a little too fast, a little too forcefully. "It's *oll recht* to be disappointed," he said.

Amanda's eyes swung to his. He could not tell if she was relieved or hurt. "Does that mean you understand that this is about more to me than just a competition? Because you didn't yesterday."

"I don't know what you're thinking because you don't tell me."

"I did in my letters, but you seem to have forgotten them."

A voice boomed on a loudspeaker and David stopped to listen. He missed the first part of the announcement, but caught the part about the show starting soon. He glanced at his goats. Were they ready? Was he forgetting anything?

"Never mind," Amanda said.

"Sorry, I'm not ignoring you," David said. "But they're about to start the show."

"Don't apologize." She nodded toward his goats in the pen beside them. "This is what matters right now."

David swallowed hard. He almost turned away, but pushed himself to be brave instead. "I haven't forgotten those letters, Amanda."

She stared into his eyes. He could sense so much emotion hiding behind that careful expression. "I haven't, either."

Neither of them spoke for a moment. David wanted to ease closer to her. He wanted to lift his hand and touch the face of the woman he had fallen for when they'd been pen pals. He could see that woman now, in Amanda's dark eyes, even though she had tried to hide her thoughts from him. He wondered if he dared to tell her how he felt. He didn't want to stand against her anymore. He wanted to stand with her.

A billy goat rammed the pen with his head, making the fence shake. Amanda's attention shot from David to the animal. "It's okay, little guy," she said and dropped down on one knee. "No need to get all worked up, ain't so?" The goat bleated and rubbed his face against the fence. Amanda reached her fingers through and scratched his neck. "These are your goats?"

"*Ya.*" David had been leaning with one hip against the fence and he straightened up. The moment was gone, replaced with the need to impress her. He wished he didn't care what she thought. But her opinion would matter more than the judges', if there weren't a contract on the line.

Amanda stood up, rested her forearms against the top of the fence and studied the goats in silence for a while. Then she pushed back and nodded her head. "I'm impressed."

David's heart leaped right into his throat. "You are?"

"Sure. You've got a *gut* herd. I thought you might need help today, or some extra support or something. But you don't. You've got this."

"I, uh, didn't expect to hear you say that."

Amanda raised her eyebrows. "You already thought your goats were the best, *ya*?"

David looked away. "I've worked hard but…" He should keep up the wall that he had been building ever since he met Amanda in person. If he told the truth then he would be vulnerable and exposed. She could twist the knife that he already felt from the rest of the world. He forced himself to be brave and plunged ahead. "I'm not so sure I can pull this off, I guess."

Amanda stared at him for a moment. "What?" she finally said.

"You heard me."

"You don't sound like the David I know. You've been acting like a know-it-all since we met."

"You sure you're not thinking of yourself?"

Amanda studied him for a few beats. "Fine. Maybe a little. But it's because I *do* know a lot. And if I don't tell people, they won't believe me."

"I believed you."

"You believed M.M., not me."

David sighed. "Maybe I did believe you, Amanda, but I didn't want you to know that."

Amanda took a step closer. She had to tilt her chin higher in order to keep eye contact. "Why not?"

"*Vell*, you haven't made it easy. All that talk about being the best, acting so *gut* at everything."

"I wasn't acting! I can't help it if I'm *gut* at something. And I shouldn't have to hide it just because it scares suitors away—" Amanda clamped her mouth shut before she finished the sentence. Her cheeks flushed red. She backed away a step and stumbled over a metal pail. It clanged against the concrete floor and she nearly fell. He caught her by the arm to steady her. She opened her mouth, but no words came out.

David made sure she was steady, then let go of her arm. "Are you calling me a suitor?" he asked as she stared up at him. It was too direct. He never should have asked. But she had been the one to bring it up, even if it had been an accident. Did she want him to court her? That had made sense when she was just good old M.M. But Amanda? He wasn't so sure about that.

Unless she had been feeling the same frustration and fear that he had. Was she just as insecure about their relationship as he was? It didn't seem possible. She was too confident. Too perfect at everything she did. What did she have to be insecure about?

Her letters came flooding back to him. Of course she was insecure. She had been telling him so, for months. He just hadn't completely understood. Then, when he'd met the real Amanda, she had seemed like a completely different person and he had shoved all memories of M.M. aside.

"*Nee*," Amanda sputtered. She took another jerky step back. "Of course not. We can barely stand to be in the same room as one another. And…and…" Amanda's voice rose, as if she couldn't stop herself. "And you don't appreciate the real me!" She spun around and fled before giving him a chance to respond.

"Amanda!" he shouted after her, but the crowd swallowed her up and she was gone.

Amanda could not believe what she had done. How could she have let those words slip out? There was no way that David wanted to court her. Why had she made it sound like she wanted him to? It had taken all her strength to let go of the jealousy and insecurity and show up today. Then she went and ruined everything by sounding like a pathetic spinster who nobody wanted to court. Sure, she was too young to be a spinster yet. But it was only a matter of time. L.D. had been her last hope.

The world blurred around her as she rushed away. Vendors called out to her and people chatted with one another. Announcements blared over the loudspeaker. A baby cried. A group of spectators clapped while a man handed a blue ribbon to a girl with long braids and a bright yellow dress. The noise made Amanda feel small and overwhelmed. She squeezed her eyes shut and told herself it was fine.

But it wasn't. She had just given away how she really felt, and to David, of all people, the one person she really wanted to impress. The one person she had thought might see and appreciate her for who she really was.

She remembered the look of shock on his face when she had mentioned the word *suitor*. Then he had mocked her by asking her if that was what she thought of him. Her fingers curled into fists. It was just too humiliating. Of course he didn't see her that way. She had allowed herself to hope for what she could never have. She had known better, but had let it happen anyway.

Amanda circled past a pen of dairy cattle with soft eyes and wet noses, a row of hutches filled with fat, fluffy rabbits and a pen full of bleating sheep before finding herself at the goats again. Amanda sighed. How had her feet carried her back here? She eased closer, but couldn't see past the row of people in front of her. She was too short, of course. Amanda shuffled to the side to catch a peek between an *Englischer* wearing a flannel shirt and an Amish man in a black coat and black felt hat. The competitors were leading their goats in a circle around the ring. She scanned the group until her eyes landed on David. The white paper taped to his back read 2350. The goat beside him was a fine-looking Angora with a thick and silky cream-colored coat.

"Number 2350, step forward," the loudspeaker boomed. Amanda held her breath. The judges were singling David out. Was he moving to the next round or being eliminated? David looked just as unsure. He frowned as he led his goat a few steps closer to the judges. A woman holding a clipboard and wearing blue jeans, a red blouse and matching red cowboy boots nodded, then stooped down to take a closer look at the mohair coat. She ran her hand down the goat's back, then straightened up and said something to a man beside her. He nodded.

"Number 3678, step forward," the man said into a microphone. A young woman wearing a cowboy hat beamed as she led a cashmere goat with a satiny white coat closer to the judges. The two judges spoke quietly to one another, then circled around the goat. The woman in red made a few notes on her clipboard, then tapped the paper with the tip of her pen. "We have a winner," the woman said. Amanda's heart sped up as she stared at David. His expression was hard to read, but she could make out the anxiety in his eyes, though he seemed to be trying to hide it.

He glanced into the crowd opposite her and Amanda watched a middle-aged man and woman wave at him. A girl stood between them, holding their hands, jumping up and down and grinning. David gave them a grim smile before turning his attention back to the judges. That must be his family, Amanda thought. A pang went through her as she watched the love in their eyes. She tried not to think about her parents, but at moments like this, the loss came rushing to the surface. What would it be like for her parents to watch her succeed? She wanted so badly to make them proud and to carry on their legacy, even though they were not here to see it.

The middle-aged woman's eyes shined as she watched David. Her lips moved and Amanda thought she must be saying a silent prayer for her son. Amanda whispered her own prayer for him. Suddenly, she realized how badly she wanted him to win. All of L.D.'s letters came flooding back to her. He wanted this, even if he didn't admit it. Or he needed it, at least. She knew what it was like to go for a hard-to-get contract. That churning anxiety had kept her up many nights. David must be feeling that now. She held her breath and waited for the big announcement.

"Congratulations to number 3678," the judge said with a smile. "You are our winner."

Amanda felt herself exhale. David should have won. It wasn't fair.

She knew how hard he had worked for this. And his Angora was beautiful. But the cashmere was nice too. It had been a tough competition. She studied David's expression as he congratulated the winner. His eyes were kind, his smile genuine. He was a better sport than she was. But she could see the tightness around his eyes. He was disappointed, that was clear to her, but only because she knew him well.

Yes, she did know him. He had seemed like a stranger after they met in person, but now she could see the real David—the man who had called himself L.D.

An *Englischer* in overalls sidestepped in front of her, and Amanda lost her view of David. She was too short to see above the crowd, so she pushed through them to get to him. "Excuse me," she said as she wound past an *Englisch* family, then inched around a heavy-set Amish man. When she pushed her way into the ring, David's family was already there. His mother hugged him while his father gave him a strong pat on the shoulder and the girl who must be his sister kneeled down to pet the goat.

David's attention shot to Amanda as soon as she appeared. The smile he had been wearing for his family faded. Their eyes met and Amanda could sense the frustration. "You had the best goat," she said as she stared up at him.

"I did?"

Amanda grinned. "Didn't you already know that?"

David shrugged. "*Ach, vell...*"

They both remembered that his family was there and David cleared his throat as he tore his gaze from hers. "This is my friend Amanda. She raises goats too. And these are my parents, Lloyd and Lydia."

"Nice to meet you, Amanda," Lydia said.

"You must be the Amanda who has been giving David *gut* advice," Lloyd said.

Amanda was surprised. She glanced at David and he smiled. "*Ya*, she is."

The girl looked up from where she kneeled on the ground, still petting the goat. "Don't forget about me. I'm Katie, David's sister."

"Hi Katie. Nice to meet you."

Katie squinted up at Amanda. "Where are your goats?"

Amanda shook her head. "They're back at my farm. I didn't show them today."

"But if she had, she would have won," David cut in. "She's got the best goats in Lancaster County for certain sure."

Amanda's chest warmed. She could tell that he meant the words. "*Danki*, David. That means a lot."

"I know it does," he said softly.

Lloyd and Lydia exchanged a glance. "Katie's been waiting to go on the rides," Lydia said. She and Lloyd moved their attention back to their son. "We'll take her and meet you over there, okay, David? You two take some time to catch up, *ya*?"

"Uh, *ya*, sure." David's voice faded away as his eyes moved back to Amanda. "I'll find you." He was looking at Amanda, even though he was still talking to his parents.

Amanda heard them murmur as they walked away and she could feel her cheeks heat. It was obvious that there was something between her and David. She just wished she knew what it was. His parents seemed pretty certain about it, but that didn't mean that David agreed. She felt a flush of embarrassment. "I meant what I said about your goat being the best."

David smiled and stepped closer. "And I meant what I said about *your* goats being the best."

They both smiled as they stared into one another's eyes.

"So, you finally admit that I'm the best at farming?" Amanda said.

"And you admit that I'm the best?" David's voice held a gentle, teasing tone. His eyes were tender and knowing.

"I never said that," Amanda murmured as she eased closer.

"*Vell, best* means better than you," David said, eyes still tender.

"Mmm." Amanda tried to think of something clever to say, but her mind was too fuzzy, her chest too hot. Her thoughts felt strange and slow. The sounds of voices, bleating and stomping hooves died away, until it was just the two of them, alone in the arena. All that existed was

David, standing in front of her, looking down into her eyes with that arresting, affectionate gaze.

"I'm glad you came back," David said.

"I couldn't stay away."

"From seeing the competition?" David swallowed hard as he stared into her eyes.

Amanda hesitated. "From seeing you."

"It didn't feel right to be here without you," David said.

"So, you admit that you wanted my help."

Amanda thought he would smile and tease her back, but his expression remained serious. "More than that. I wanted your company. I missed you, M.M."

Amanda understood exactly what he meant. Nothing had been the same since they had met in person. It had been hard losing the friend who had written to her nearly every day. "I missed you too," Amanda whispered. She licked her lips. All she could think about was how much she wanted him to lean down and kiss her. But that was impossible. They were in the middle of the ring, with crowds of people milling around them. Her heart thudded into her throat. He reached out and took her hand. The touch felt comforting and right and it sent a wave of joy shimmering through her.

"Do you think we could be friends again?" he asked.

"Yes." The word left her lips automatically, before she could think. She wanted to ask him if he wanted to be more than friends. Friends didn't hold hands like this, after all. And the space between friends didn't glimmer with expectation as it did right now. But the question stuck in her throat and she just stared up at him instead. She could not think straight. All she could do was hold his hand and hope for the promise of something more between them.

"Amanda?"

"*Ya?*" Amanda's heart pounded with expectation. He was going to ask if he could court her. Wasn't he? Every muscle strained with hope. This was the moment she had been waiting for all these months.

"Amanda, would you—"

"All contestants please clear the ring," a voice boomed over the loudspeaker.

Amanda jumped.

David's attention jerked to the people nearby. A handful of farmers were leading dairy goats toward them. His Angora bleated and pulled against her lead.

He dropped Amanda's hand. "We should go."

"*Recht.* Of course." Amanda felt as if she'd been caught, even though she'd done nothing wrong. Why had she let herself get so carried away, right there, in the middle of the showgrounds? Because when David was nearby, everything else faded away, that was why. And it was time she admitted it to herself. And maybe to him too.

Chapter Eight

Amanda woke up the next morning knowing exactly what she would do. Naomi stopped her as she tried to sneak out the front door while the rest of the family was eating breakfast.

"Where are you running off to?" Naomi asked with narrowed eyes.

"Nowhere."

Naomi ran her gaze down Amanda's neatly ironed purple dress. "You're not going to see to the goats in your Sunday best, that's certain sure."

"*Nee*, I've already done the chores."

Naomi turned her head toward the kitchen door. "Amanda's sneaking away and she doesn't want us to know where she's going!" she shouted.

Amanda groaned. "Naomi, I'm going to get you back for that."

Naomi just grinned.

Silverware clanged, wooden chairs scraped against floorboards, bare feet pounded across the kitchen, then Benjamin, Miriam and Leah appeared in the doorway. "What's going on?" Leah asked.

"Ask her," Naomi said.

"Nothing is going on," Amanda said.

"Then why are you sneaking out alone?" Miriam asked.

"Because it's a visiting Sunday," Amanda said.

"That doesn't explain why you're going without us," Benjamin said.

"Where's Amanda going without us?" Emma asked as she rounded the kitchen doorway and hurried down the hallway to them.

Amanda sighed and leaned against the wall. They were not going to let her leave without a full explanation. "Why do you all have to be so nosy?"

"Because that's our job," Benjamin said as he grinned and patted her head.

"Don't pat me on the head," Amanda said.

"You'll miss me someday," Benjamin said.

"Today is not that day," Amanda said.

Miriam waved her hand to silence them. "So where are you going?"

"Out?"

"Obviously." Miriam put her hands on her hips. "Out where?"

"Um…"

Benjamin winked at Emma. "Our plan worked."

"What do you mean?" Amanda tried to act surprised.

"Our plan to get you and David together."

"I never said that I'm going to David's."

"Where else would you go without telling us?"

"Lots of places."

Benjamin chuckled. "Right. So, are you courting yet?"

"Shouldn't he be coming here to pick you up?" Naomi asked.

"I made a shoofly pie last night," Emma said. "Invite him in for some when he comes to get you."

"*Nee.* He's not coming here."

"He should," Miriam said. "Isn't it a long drive over to his place?"

"I'm going to visit his farm. I want to see it."

"So you *are* going to see him," Miriam cut in.

"Did you just fool me into admitting that?"

Miriam smiled. "I did."

"So are you courting or not?" Naomi asked.

"Does it matter?" Amanda asked.

"*Ya!*" her siblings shouted in unison.

"It'll be the biggest news to hit the Amish telegraph in years," Benjamin said. "'Amanda Stoltzfus Finds a Suitor.' No one will believe it."

Amanda shot him a look. "Enough, Benji."

"Just wait until he shows up to drive you home from the next church meeting. Or will he take you to a service over in his church district?"

"You're getting way ahead of yourself."

"I'm not the one sneaking off to see a suitor."

Amanda squeezed her eyes shut. "Benjamin, you are impossible."

"Thank you."

Emma laughed. "Benji, you're going to push her too far one of these days."

"Hey, if it weren't for me, they wouldn't be courting. I was the one who made sure that Miriam asked him for lunch, wasn't I?"

"We are not courting," Amanda said. "I already told you that."

"Then maybe you shouldn't go visiting over there," Miriam said. "It might be too forward."

"*Nee*, it's fine. We're friends."

"So, he's expecting you?"

"Um… Maybe."

Miriam raised an eyebrow.

"It's fine, Miriam."

"I'll go with you," Miriam said. She reached for her black Sunday cloak on the peg beside the door.

"*Nee!*" Amanda said, a little too loudly.

Miriam's hand froze above her cloak.

"I mean, there's no need. His parents and sister will be there. He's asked me to visit his farm." She paused before mumbling, "Just not today, necessarily."

Miriam turned away from her cloak. "Just not today? Is that what you said?"

"It was an open invitation."

Miriam studied Amanda's expression for a moment. "Okay. But don't stay too long. You don't want to give the wrong idea."

"You all were trying to play matchmaker a couple days ago, and now you're trying to discourage me?"

"I'm not discouraging you. I just want to make sure you're not getting ahead of yourself. There's a proper way to do this."

"We've been writing for months." Amanda started to say more, but stopped herself. A few days ago, she had been trying to convince them that she and David weren't interested in one another. Now she was trying to convince them of the opposite? It made no sense. What was happening to her?

David Troyer, that was what.

Amanda sighed and slipped closer toward the door. "It's fine." She eased it open and began to slip outside. "It's not a big deal, really. I've been meaning to visit his farm for a while. You know, to see the goats."

"Right, the goats," Miriam deadpanned.

"I knew it was a *gut* match, Amanda!" Benjamin said as Amanda crept onto the porch. He turned to Naomi. "Didn't I?"

"We all did!" Naomi said.

"It'll be wedding season soon!" Benjamin added.

Amanda could imagine the sly grin on his face, but she did not turn around to see it. She was already hurrying down the porch steps. If she listened to her siblings, she might lose her nerve. She had to push herself, even though she was anxious. Yesterday's encounter with David was still burned in her mind. She was almost certain that he had been about to ask to court her. She could not wait another day to find out for sure.

It didn't take long for the doubt to creep in. The drive to David's farm was a long one, and she had plenty of time to think. Her thoughts wandered as Clyde trotted along the side of the highway and cars zipped past, whipping up wind and tangling her *kapp* strings. She wondered what would have happened if she had stayed a little longer at the fair yesterday. After they were interrupted, Amanda had hurried home. She had been too flustered to stay, especially with David's cheeks flushed red and him looking as if he was having second thoughts about what he had been about to say to her.

But he had just been nervous, right? That was what she had convinced herself as she tossed and turned all night long, trying to decide what to do. As the sun rose, she had decided to take control of the situation. She was not one to wait around. She liked to act. It made sense to go to him and see what he had to say. But what if David regretted the moment they'd had—or had almost had—together? After all, he had clammed up pretty quickly, then made an excuse about needing to get his goats loaded onto the *Englisch* driver's trailer. Or maybe he really had needed to load them. She didn't know.

Which was why she was determined to find out the truth today.

But as the buggy wheels ground over the pavement and sunshine flooded the pastureland surrounding her, Amanda's doubts continued to deepen. What if Miriam was right? What if she was being too forward? David was not expecting her. And he had seemed pretty reluctant for her to visit when she had mentioned it Friday on the hillside. He *had* apologized and told her that she was welcome. But what if he had just been trying to spare her feelings? What if she had misread him at the show and he was not happy to see her today?

Amanda frowned and tugged the reins as they came to a stop sign. "Whoa," she said, then looked both ways before slapping the reins. "Walk on." Clyde's heavy hooves began to beat their steady rhythm again. Amanda watched as they neared a white farmhouse with a white barn bordered by several acres of cornfields. A handful of buggies were parked alongside the road and a group of *youngies* tossed a volleyball back and forth over a net. An older woman stood on the farmhouse porch watching them while a toddler clung to her leg. Amanda waved and the woman waved back. It would be fine, Amanda told herself. It was a visiting Sunday. Everyone was out visiting today. David wouldn't think it was strange if she showed up. Or at least, that was what she told herself as her heart thudded faster with every mile.

David Troyer was kicking himself. Why had he let Amanda leave the show without telling her how he felt? He had been so close to letting it all spill out. The moment had felt so right, as if no one else had been inside the big sheet-metal building with them. Just him and the woman he loved… He cut himself off. His thoughts were getting away from him. Did he love Amanda? He had loved M.M. That he did know. And he knew that being around Amanda had been doing strange things to him. His stomach dropped every time he saw her. And then his heart would speed up until he wanted to run away and hide from whatever was happening inside of him. Something was going on, that was for certain sure. But Amanda was not easy to read, like M.M. had been. He had to figure out how to put the two together in a way that made sense. Which was more difficult than it sounded.

"Are you feeling *oll recht*?" David's mother was watching him as she slowly sipped from her coffee mug and his father flipped through *The Budget* newspaper on the couch beside her.

His head jerked up to stare at her. "Uh, *ya*, of course."

"*Vell*, you've been staring into nothing for so long that your *kaffi* has gotten cold."

David had not realized that he had been so zoned out.

"I know who he's thinking about!" Katie said as she looked up. She lay propped on her elbows on the living room floor, beside a pile of markers and an open coloring book. "That woman at the show yesterday. The one he wouldn't stop talking to."

David flinched. Was it that obvious? Judging by his mother's smile, it was.

His father folded the paper and set it down on the end table. "Amanda, wasn't it?"

"*Ya*. But we're just friends."

His mother and father raised their eyebrows in unison, which would have been funny if David had been in the mood to laugh about it.

"Really. We're friends." It felt good to be able to say it. He was overjoyed that Amanda had said that she was his friend yesterday, after he had gotten up the courage to ask her how she felt. But it didn't seem like enough anymore. He wanted to court her. He wanted to be with her every day. He wanted to watch the sunsets with her, to hold her hand while they walked their farms together, to tease her and watch her eyes flash when she had a witty retort. He had been so caught up in his feelings that he had almost kissed her, right there at the fair, without caring who was watching.

"Aren't you going to court her?" Katie asked as she picked up a green marker.

"*Ach*, I don't know." David shifted in his seat. "It's hard to know what she wants."

"Is it?" Lydia asked.

David frowned. "*Vell*, yes."

"All you have to do is ask her. Have you done that?"

David set down the mug of coffee that had gone cold in his hands. It hit the end table with a gentle thump. "Maybe not exactly."

"It's not that complicated. Just communicate with her.

Be open about how you feel and encourage her to do the same."

"I don't know if she'd like that."

"Only one way to find out," Lloyd said.

"Worst that can happen is that you find out she doesn't want to be courted. Better to know now and move on."

David frowned. It could be worse than that. She could tell him that she saw right through him, to all his failures. She could remind him that he didn't know what he was doing and that his decisions had left his farm on the verge of collapse. She could tell him that he simply wasn't good enough for her. There was too much at stake to be straightforward.

"She came to support you yesterday," Lydia said. "That says a lot."

"*Ya*, but I'm afraid that she was more interested in seeing the competition. She's a serious farmer."

"Both things can be true, you know," Lydia said. "She could have gone to see the competition and to support you."

Lloyd nodded. "People are complicated."

"Tell me about it," David muttered under his breath. Everything his parents said made sense, but he knew that as soon as he saw Amanda again, reason and logic would go out the window. All he would be able to think about would be her and how she sent a flurry of butterflies through his belly.

A knock sounded on the front door.

"A visitor," Lydia said. She smiled, stood up and straightened her apron. "I'll get it. Might be the bishop's wife. Last time I saw her, she mentioned she might bring by a new pie recipe she's trying out."

David felt a jolt of hope zip through him at the sound of the door. What if it were… No, that was silly of him. Why would Amanda drive all the way out here?

Because she felt the same way about him as he did about her.

The thought made him stand up fast, his pulse pounding in his throat. He shouldn't let himself get carried away. It might not be completely proper for Amanda to come to his house. Folks might say it was too forward of her. He should have gone over to hers. That would be the right way to do things. If he weren't such a coward, he would have.

He could hear the front door open and close, followed by the muffled sound of women's voices. He stood waiting, telling himself to stop being as silly as a schoolboy with a crush. Footsteps padded down the hallway and the living room door swung open. Amanda stood in the doorway. David's heart plunged into his stomach, then bounced back into his chest. She had come to see him. Her cheeks were bright and she held her hands clasped in front of her as her eyes darted from one person to another. Neither of them spoke for a moment.

Katie looked up from her coloring book. "Hi, Amanda!"

"I'll get you a cup of *kaffi*," Lydia said from the hallway.

"*Danki*," Amanda said. Her voice was much softer than usual.

"I'm so glad you're here," David said as soon as he could find the words.

Their eyes met and the tension melted from her face. "I, uh, know you weren't expecting me."

"It's a visiting Sunday," Lloyd said. "We're not expecting anybody in particular. Folks just show up, ain't so?"

Amanda smiled. "*Ya.* That's true."

"*Kumme* sit." Lloyd motioned to the chair beside David.

David patted the seat. He was still looking at her, and their eyes locked again. A shimmer of warmth rippled through him. It felt so right for Amanda to be here in his living room, with his family. She looked like she belonged with them. Amanda's eyes sparkled and he sensed that she felt the same. Or at least he hoped she did. She was here, after all. And the way she was looking at him…

Amanda dropped her gaze to Katie's picture as she made her way to the chair. "That looks nice," she said.

"*Danki.* It's a barn, but I colored it green instead of white or red because I like green best. Do you like green best?"

"I do like green."

Katie set down the marker and closed her coloring book. "We were just talking about you and then you showed up. That's kind of funny, isn't it?"

Amanda froze. "You were talking about me?" She stared at Katie, then turned to look at David. He felt his face heat. Then, as if she just realized that she was still standing, Amanda sat down a little too quickly. The chair creaked at the impact.

"*Ach*, not really," David said.

Amanda's forehead creased. She glanced at Lloyd, then back to David.

"*Ya*, we were," Katie said. "*Mamm* and *Daed* asked if David is courting you. And then he said *nee*, you two are just friends."

"*Nee*, that's not what we said." David could not believe that Katie had just said that. And right when it seemed like things were beginning to work out for them.

Katie squinted her eyes. "That is too what you said."

"*Vell*, not in that order." David shook his head. "You're mixing everything up."

Katie shrugged. "You still said it."

Lloyd frowned at his daughter. "Katie, that's enough."

"I don't understand. You always tell me to tell the truth and that's what I'm doing."

Lloyd rubbed his temples. "*Ya*, but…"

"I've got *kaffi*," Lydia said as she bustled into the room. "And a tin of ginger snaps. Katie and I did some baking." Lydia handed Amanda the mug then glanced around the room. "You all are awfully quiet. What did I miss?"

"I was just telling Amanda—" Katie started to say.

"No need to repeat it," Lloyd interrupted.

Katie heaved a dramatic sigh. "*Oll recht.* Not sure what's so wrong about telling the truth."

"Nothing," Lloyd and Lydia said at the same time.

"But sometimes it can be more complicated than that," Lloyd added.

Amanda held the coffee mug in two hands as she stared into it. There was a long, awkward silence. "I should go." She set down her mug on a crocheted coaster. "I'm sorry to have barged in like this."

"Barged in?" Lydia shook her head. "Don't be ridiculous. We're so happy to see you. It was lovely meeting you yesterday."

"Don't mind us," Lloyd said. "Sometimes we say more

than we should around here, but only with the best intentions, right Katie?"

"Right," Katie said and grinned.

"Why don't you show Amanda around the farm?" Lydia asked. "I'm sure she'd like to see your goats." She turned her attention to Amanda. "David was just telling us that you are a serious farmer with a *gut* head for business."

Amanda's entire demeanor changed, as if a light had switched on from the inside. "He did?"

"Of course I did," David said.

Amanda turned to look at him. He had never seen such a genuine grin in his life before. "Oh," she said. Then repeated "Oh," as if she was still processing what she had heard.

"David couldn't stop talking about your farm after he visited the other day," Katie said.

"It must be a well-run operation," Lloyd said. "David said it's the best goat farm in the county."

"Oh," Amanda said once again. She was still grinning. "*Vell*, maybe I could stay for a tour of your lovely farm."

Lydia chuckled. "Are you surprised to hear what David's been saying about you?"

"Maybe a little bit."

David stood up. He didn't want his mother to ask too many questions. They might all figure out how insecure he had been these last few days. "Let's start with the barn, *ya*?"

"Sure." Amanda picked her mug back up, took a quick sip of coffee, then followed him to the door, mug in hand.

"We'll have lunch when you get back," Lydia said.

"But take your time." She glanced at Lloyd and they exchanged a knowing look. "No need to hurry."

"*Ya*, no need to hurry back," Lloyd repeated.

David shook his head as he grabbed his straw hat from the peg on the wall of the entryway. His parents were not subtle people. "They had a lot to say," David said as he opened the door and motioned for Amanda to go ahead of him. A warm breeze drifted toward him, carrying the scent of fresh cut grass and damp earth.

"*Vell*, I liked hearing it." Amanda turned to give him a sly look.

David's heart skipped a beat. He tried to give her a debonair expression but grinned instead. He was just too happy. Everything was working out in ways he had not believed possible. Sure, he and Amanda had not had a chance to talk about the future, or how they really felt, but things were moving forward, for certain sure. She was no longer a rival. She was a friend. And, hopefully, things would keep getting better from there.

"So, this is the farm," David said as they stepped off the front stoop and into the yard. He gave a nervous laugh. "But I guess that's obvious." His first instinct was to feel inadequate. His farm was small and barely profitable. It was nothing compared to hers. But he squared his shoulders and reminded himself that it was enough. He worked hard and it showed. He didn't need to be ashamed just because his place was smaller. The outbuildings were freshly painted, the dirt was raked clean and the chicken coop had just been mucked out. He pointed to a white shed. "That's where we keep the goats." It wasn't as big as a barn, but it was good enough. Goats foraged on weeds, grass and dandelions in a series of pens in the yard and nearby field. The buggy horse was stabled in an adjacent building, which was just large enough for one stall, the winter hay and the tack. A white wooden fence surrounded the tidy property, with green rolling hills rising in the background. In the distance, a one-room Amish schoolhouse stood between a pear orchard and a cornfield.

"I want to get a closer look at the goats," Amanda said as she took off toward the shed.

"I thought you would." David trotted behind her. "Do you, uh, like what you see so far?"

"Absolutely. It's a well-run farm, for certain sure." She glanced over her shoulder at him without slowing down. "And you do most of the work yourself?"

"*Ya. Daed*'s got an old back injury, so he can't do much. *Mamm* works out here when she's not busy with the housework, and Katie does some farm chores after school. But it's mostly me."

"I'm fortunate to have all my siblings to help. It's never too much for any of us, when we're all working together."

"My farm is small enough that I can handle it on my own."

"You told me in one of your letters that it was in bad shape when you bought it. Looks like you've really turned it around."

David rubbed the back of his neck. He could get used to all the compliments. "*Ach*, I've done some work on it."

Amanda laughed. "I remember your description. You've done a lot more than 'some work' on it."

David beamed. "*Ya.* I guess you're right."

Amanda caught his eye. Her gaze was warm and full

of mirth. "I better stop now or it'll go straight to your head."

"No fear of that. You've put me down enough since we've met to keep me humble for the rest of my life."

Amanda laughed again. "You're exaggerating."

David raised an eyebrow.

"You are!"

He lifted his hand and made a pinching gesture with his thumb and pointer finger, leaving just a sliver of space between them. "Maybe just a little."

"More than that."

David smiled and dropped his hand. "I think it's time we call a truce and start over."

Amanda's grin faded, but the warmth in her eyes did not. She bit her lip, looked down, then back up at David. "I think I'd like that."

He had never wanted to hug anyone more than in that moment. Amanda looked so sincere and nervous, which was exactly how he felt. Something was stirring between them and he liked it. The closeness made him feel giddy inside.

David wasn't sure what to say after that, so he was glad when Amanda turned toward the goat pen and broke the silence. She motioned toward the Angoras. "That's *gut* mohair. You should have won the show."

A zip of anticipation danced through him. "In all the excitement after you showed up, I forgot—" David stopped himself. He didn't want to sound too eager. "I mean, there's been so much to say since you arrived, I haven't really had a chance to tell you. I've got *wunderbar* news."

"You do?"

David nodded. "Sure do." He exhaled and looked out at his goats. This was the moment he had been waiting for ever since he'd started writing to Amanda. He was finally going to get to share his success with her. "I got the contract."

Amanda gasped. "You did?"

"Yup." David grinned. He knew he must look like a boy on Christmas morning, but he didn't care. He was too happy to be self-conscious.

"When?"

"They approached me after the show, as I was loading up my goats."

"Even though you didn't get first place."

"They said my farm had what they were looking for. It didn't matter what the judges thought. What mattered was the quality of the mohair and that I could produce enough for them. Oh, and that I was willing to give them an exclusive contract."

"You did it!" Amanda launched herself at David, and his arms automatically folded around her. He didn't even have time to be shocked. They were both too caught up in the moment. They were laughing out loud and Amanda was squeezing him as hard as she could, which wasn't very hard, but he could tell how happy she was for him. It felt like the best celebration he had ever experienced, just the two of them alone in the farmyard, holding one another and shouting.

Amanda broke away and stepped back. Her face was flushed and her brown eyes sparkled. "Which company is it?"

"Oh, right. That's the best part. Lancaster Fleece &

Fiber! Can you believe it? Everyone wants that contract, ain't so?"

Amanda's expression shifted. "*Ya.* Everyone." She stared up at him. The sparkle in her eyes had vanished. "Including me."

David wasn't sure how to respond. He was happy he'd gotten the contract. He needed it. But he didn't want to beat Amanda for it. He would have wanted that a few days ago, but everything felt different now.

"I didn't know you were trying to get it too,"

"I wasn't." Amanda inhaled, then exhaled slowly. "I *had* the contract. You just took it from me."

David's joy evaporated. Suddenly, nothing was okay anymore. He had taken something away from Amanda that he could not afford to give back, something that had been a part of her identity. He didn't know what to do or how to fix it, even though he desperately wanted to.

Chapter Nine

Amanda felt like the earth was no longer solid beneath her feet. Lancaster Fleece & Fiber had warned her that they might pull the contract. The company was under new management, and they wanted to go in a new direction, consider other farms, other options. She had been negotiating with them and it was clear that they did not appreciate her family's history with the company. Even so, she'd never believed that they would actually refuse to renew their contract with Stoneybrook Farm. They'd said it wasn't personal, but business *was* personal to her. Hadn't she proven that she could produce for them? How could this happen on her watch? How could she fail her family like this?

Lancaster Fleece & Fiber was Stoneybrook Farm's biggest contract. By far. Her brain began to run the numbers automatically. Could the family business keep going without those biannual bulk purchases from Lancaster Fleece & Fiber? Yes. There were still the dairy profits. But this was going to hurt. She had no other buyers lined up. And why should she? Lancaster Fleece & Fiber had always been loyal and fair, until they'd changed ownership last spring.

"Amanda?"

Her attention jerked back to David.

"Are you *oll recht*?"

"*Ya*. Of course." She reached out and grasped a fence post for support as she told herself to get it together. "I, uh, should probably get home. Just need to run some numbers."

"But it's Sunday. You can't today."

"Right. No working on Sunday." Nothing was making sense anymore. Her ears were buzzing and David's voice sounded far away.

"Amanda. Sit down." He grabbed a plastic feed bucket and turned it upside down. "Here."

"What? *Nee*, I'm okay."

"You're pale as a sheet."

She sank down onto the feed bucket.

"Didn't you know that they were giving the contract to someone else?"

Amanda thought back to the blinking red light on the answering machine in the processing building. Her church district allowed telephones in family businesses, but she had not checked the messages yesterday, when she should have. She had been too eager to get to the agricultural fair. And, if she were honest, she had been too afraid that it would be bad news. The negotiations with Lancaster Fiber & Fleece had not been going well. Even so, she had not thought this could really happen. "*Nee*. I didn't know. They may have left a message on my answering machine, but I haven't listened to it yet."

"But you knew they were considering going with someone else?"

"*Ya*. But I certain sure didn't know it was you."

"It isn't personal. I fought hard for it. I was pretty desperate."

Amanda heard the word *desperate*, but it didn't register. All she could think about was that she had lost her family's biggest single contract. Her parents' legacy was in danger. Her siblings would lose respect for her. She would look like a failure to everyone. They would think that the suitors who had told her to give up farm management for housework were right.

"Amanda, what are you thinking right now?"

David kneeled down on one knee so that he was on eye level with her. His gaze was steady and searching.

"That everyone will think…" She shook her head. "Never mind. It doesn't matter."

"It must. I can see how upset you are."

Amanda swallowed hard. She dropped her eyes to study her hands. "Have you ever felt desperate to prove to everyone that you're good at something? That *Gott* made you to do something, even though it isn't expected, and sometimes not even accepted?"

David sighed. He reached out and put his big, rough hand over hers. She waited for him to speak, but he did not.

A goat bleated in the pen and a dog barked in the distance. The plastic bucket dug into Amanda's thighs, but she didn't get up.

"I'm sorry," David said finally.

Amanda shook her head. "Don't be. You won fair and square."

"I wish I hadn't."

"You don't mean that."

David looked away. "I do and I don't. I need the contract, Amanda."

"So do I," she said softly.

Another long moment passed. A nanny goat reached her head through the fence and tried to nip at the overturned feed bucket. Amanda scratched the goat beneath her chin. "I'm going to have to try to win the contract back. I'm sorry, David. It's not personal. It's business." Amanda didn't feel right about it. She wanted to celebrate with him. She wanted to go inside, eat lunch with his family, then sit by the woodstove while nibbling gingersnaps and discussing his future business plans.

But she couldn't. She had to think about her own family and her own farm. David had become a friend, but that was all he was. He wasn't family. She owed her allegiance to her own flesh and blood. They depended on her and they depended on this contract. Amanda stood up. "I'm sorry. I should go."

"You don't have to do that."

"I think we both know that I do." She gave a weak smile. "We're rivals again now." Her heart sank as she said it. She no longer felt any satisfaction at the thought of beating him at a business deal. She wanted everything to go back to the way it had been just a few minutes ago, before she knew that her own livelihood was at risk.

"It doesn't have to be like that, Amanda."

"We don't have to fight like we used to. But how can we be friends if I'm working against you?" She shook her head. "It wouldn't be right. I would feel too guilty."

"*Nee*, you don't have to feel guilty about doing your job."

Amanda stood up and brushed off the skirt of her

dress. "I do if we're friends. Because I intend to get this contract back, no matter what it takes. It's going to hurt you, David, and there's nothing I can do to stop that. I can't…" Amanda's throat felt raw and thick. She cleared it and forced herself to go on. "I can't do that to a friend."

"Amanda, think about what you're saying. You're not making sense."

"Unfortunately, I am." She did not tell him that she wanted to be more than friends, that the emotions had been overwhelming when she had leaped into his arms and he had held her close. She'd hugged him without thinking, out of excitement. But as soon as she'd felt his warm, solid chest against her cheek, she'd been reminded that she felt much more for him than friendship. She had come here hoping that he would court her, after all.

And now, she would have to push all those feelings away again.

David didn't know how to feel as he watched Amanda's buggy wind down the driveway in a trail of dust. His emotions had swung from elation to disappointment to something he could not identify. Why did she have to fight him on this? No, that wasn't fair of him. He understood why. She had to survive, same as he did. She had responsibilities to her family too. What didn't make sense was that she refused to stay friends.

Unless…

David straightened up as he watched the horse trot onto the highway, tail and hooves raised high, the buggy jolting along behind. They had almost kissed at the agricultural fair. She had leaped into his arms today. Surely, she had felt the same connection that he did. It was more than friendship for her too. She was shutting him out because she couldn't love him and hurt him at the same time. She had to stamp out the affection that was forming between them.

David frowned and squinted into the sun to watch the buggy disappear over a distant hill. He kept staring at the horizon until a blue pickup truck crested the rise and roared down the highway toward him. He sighed and turned away. Maybe he was just hoping that was the reason why. Amanda might have been angry about losing the contract to him. And he would not blame her for that. He had stolen a big piece of her livelihood. If he had realized that Stoneybrook Farm had always held that contract, he would not have gone for it.

An uncomfortable feeling settled in his gut. He wasn't so sure that was true. It was easy to be noble when it was theoretical. If he had been offered the contract knowing that Amanda would lose it, would he really have turned it down? He hoped so, but he didn't know if he really would have, or if he even *should* have. They were not married. They were not even courting. He had to feed the ones who were dependent on him. That was the harsh truth. For both of them.

So what would happen now?

When David wandered back inside, Lydia and Katie were setting the table for five. David gave a grim shake of the head. Lydia glanced behind him to the empty hallway, furrowed her brow, then looked back at him. "By the look on your face, something's gone wrong between the two of you."

Katie placed a fork onto the table. "You're not courting yet?"

David exhaled. "*Nee*. We're not courting."

"But you will soon, ain't so? She likes the color green, same as me. I think she's nice. You should ask to take her on a buggy ride."

Lydia put a hand on Katie's shoulder. "Why don't you put the extra plate and silverware back? We won't need it anymore."

Katie sighed, but did as she was told.

"Do you want to talk about it?" Lydia asked in a low voice.

"There's nothing to talk about. We've been friends for a while, but there's too much between us…" He took off his straw hat and ran his fingers through his hair. "Some things just aren't meant to be. We aren't compatible."

"You seem to have common interests. And she came all the way here to see you today. It's been a long time since you've taken a woman on a buggy ride. Katie's idea is pretty *gut*, ain't so?"

"I wish it were that simple."

"You're not sweet on her?"

"It doesn't matter if I am or not. Some things can't work out, even if you want them to."

Lydia studied his expression for a moment, then patted his arm. "Let's see what *Gott* can do, *ya*?"

"It's probably for the best to end things between us before they start."

"*Vell*, we'll leave that to *Gott*."

"*Mamm*, why are you so insistent on trying to make a match between us? I just told you it's not a good fit."

Lydia's face tightened. She looked at her son for a moment before speaking. "You work too hard, *sohn*. And you carry too much on your shoulders. When we met

Amanda at the fair yesterday, I could see the spark between you. And then when she came visiting today, *vell*, I could tell she'd be *gut* for you. Her eyes light up when she looks at you. You need a partner. Life is hard when you're alone."

"I'm not alone. I've got you and *Daed*."

"And me!" Katie piped up from the other side of the kitchen.

"You're not supposed to be listening," David said.

"Then don't talk loudly enough for me to hear."

Lydia laughed, then pulled David into the hallway. "You'll always have us, but it isn't the same. You need a *frau*, David. Someone to work the farm with you and form a family of your own. It's time you started thinking about your own future. I can see how much Amanda loves farming. She would be a *gut* partner."

"You've barely met her."

"I trust your judgment."

"But I've never talked about her before."

Lydia smiled. "I've seen the way you look at her, same as she looks at you. Your eyes light up too."

David knew it was true, but he could not allow the conversation to keep going. Otherwise, he might jump into his buggy and race after Amanda and… And then what? There was nothing he could say. There was nothing he could do to fix the problem short of a marriage proposal. Then maybe they could merge their farms together. But it was too soon for that. And that would not even solve it, anyway. Amanda would want to keep her own farm. She wouldn't want to give it all up to move into his place. Sure, he could go to Stoneybrook Farm, but then he would be infringing on her territory and taking away her independence, which she so obviously valued. He would not do that to her. He loved her too much.

Stop. This was ridiculous. Was he really thinking about marrying Amanda?

"What is it?" Lydia asked.

David shook his head. "Nothing."

"*Ach*, it's something. I can see by the look on your face."

"It's nothing that will be solved by talking about it. Let's eat and forget you ever met Amanda."

"And you're going to try to forget you ever met her too?" Lydia's eyes narrowed.

"*Ya*. That's exactly what I'm going to do. And it's as much for her sake as it is for mine. So please just trust me and leave it be."

Lydia stared at him for a few beats before exhaling and shaking her head. "*Oll recht.* But I don't like it."

"Neither do I," David murmured, too quietly for her to hear.

David didn't sleep well that night. He tossed and turned, pulled his quilt, and punched down his pillow, but nothing worked. His thoughts were too full of Amanda. When he finally drifted off, half the night was gone. His last thought as a soft, gray haze overtook him was that it would be time for the milking soon.

His next conscious thought was confusion. Sunlight streamed through his window and Katie was screaming. Panic bolted through him. He threw off the covers, leaped out of bed and stormed out of the room in his pajamas. He did not stop to pull on his boots, but bounded out of the front door in his bare feet. "Katie!" he shouted as he jumped off the stoop and pounded across the dirt farmyard.

She stood backed against the fence inside the goat pen, a bucket of feed spilled on the ground beside her. "Skunk!" she screeched as she scrunched up against the fence. "There's a skunk in here with the goats!"

David felt a wave of relief. Katie was okay. Then a new wave of panic replaced the previous one. He had rounded up all the Angoras and put them in the pen the night before. Today he was going to start the sheering. His contract depended on the mohair in that pen—the mohair trapped alongside a skunk. "Don't move!" he shouted to Katie. He slowed his pace so he didn't scare the animal. "It won't spray you if you leave it alone." At least he hoped that was true. "Just ease out of there slowly. Without any sudden movements."

"It won't hurt me?" Katie asked.

"Nee."

"But what about the goats?"

"I'll take care of them. You come on out of there."

"Will the skunk spray them?"

"It could. But I'm going to make sure it doesn't."

"They're my goats too. I'll protect them." Katie's hands clenched into fists by her sides. She took a deep breath.

"Katie, *nee*! Don't scare the skunk!"

Katie did not listen. Instead, she burst forward, fists clenched as she shouted as loudly as she could. "Get out of here! Leave my goats alone!" She charged straight into the herd, which was tightly packed, bleating and shifting against one another nervously. They could smell the stranger among them.

"*Nee!*" David shouted. He watched, helpless, while the goats panicked, butting and stomping as they all pressed against the fence with nowhere to go. He caught sight of a black form waddling low to the ground among the hooves. With slow-motion horror, he saw the skunk shift its weight onto its front paws, lift its tail and spray.

A wave of helplessness washed over him. His knees felt weak and his breath caught in his chest. Could this really be happening? The stench hit him and he staggered backward. Katie screamed, turned on her heels and sprinted out of the goat pen. David watched as the goats bleated and kicked, the whites of their eyes showing as they struggled to get away. The skunk waddled out from among the herd, tail still raised high. It trotted out of the gate that Katie had left open and scampered away, disappearing behind the goat shed. If David didn't know any better, he would've thought the animal looked smug and satisfied, as if it had just played a good joke on them all. Well, the joke *was* on David, for sure, because now his entire stock of mohair was ruined. The realization was more than he could handle, so he just stood there, dumbstruck, unable to speak or move.

"David." Katie tugged on his hand.

He flinched as he was pulled back into the moment. He had to do something. He just didn't know what. "Are you okay, Katie?" David tore his attention from the goats to look at her.

She had pulled her apron up and was holding it over her mouth and nose. "I think so."

"It didn't get you?"

She shook her head. "It sprayed in the other direction."

Even so, the smell lingered around her. He wasn't sure if it was in the air or stuck to her clothes and hair. "Best get inside and get cleaned up."

She squeezed his hand. "I'm sorry."

David lowered himself onto one knee to see eye to eye with her. The damp earth formed a wet patch on his pants leg. It didn't matter, of course. Everything they wore would have to be washed, and perhaps burned. He wasn't sure. This wasn't something that had ever happened to him before. "Don't feel bad," David said. "You were very brave trying to protect the goats."

"I should have listened to you."

David sighed. "*Ya*, you should have. And now you've learned your lesson. But it was still brave of you."

"You're not mad?"

David hesitated. *Mad* wasn't the right word. *Devastated* was more like it. *Mad* was too shallow an emotion for what he was experiencing. He forced a sad smile. "*Nee*, I'm not mad. It's going to be *oll recht*."

"How do you know that? The goats smell terrible now."

"Because I'm going to trust *Gott*'s plan, ain't so? As Amish we believe that everything that happens is His will."

"Even getting sprayed by a skunk?"

David hesitated. The thought of losing his contract tested the limits of this belief. But he would stay strong and hold on to what he knew was true. He took a deep breath. "Even that."

"What are you going to do?" Katie asked, still pressing her apron against her nose and mouth.

"I don't know," he answered. There was only one person he knew who might be able to help him. But how could he ask Amanda for advice after he had stolen her contract?

Chapter Ten

Amanda almost didn't answer the business phone. She had just finished putting a crate of milk bottles into the propane-powered refrigerator in the production building and did not want to be bothered. She couldn't cope with having to talk to the managers at Lancaster Fleece & Fiber, if that was who was calling. She stared at the phone for a few rings. Maybe if she ignored it, all her problems would just go away. David's pained expression flashed in her mind. He had been so excited about his success. She had too, until she'd realized that his gain had been her loss. He had looked so confused and vulnerable when she announced that she had to sever their friendship. But what else could she have done? She could not hurt the man she had fallen in love with.

Yes, it was love and she knew it without question now. David wasn't the insensitive, competitive rival that she had thought he was when they first met in person. He was L.D., the man she had already fallen for. She had to force herself to pull away from him. Anything else would be too confusing and painful for both of them. She was doing it for him as much as for herself. He needed to be free to keep that contract without guilt so that he could put food on his family's table. She couldn't let him feel conflicted about his success. And she needed to be free to take it back, if at all possible. They both had to look out for themselves.

That reasoning sounded logical, but it didn't sit well. It felt wrong, deep down inside, but Amanda didn't know what else to do. She didn't feel wrong about looking out for her own family. She just wished that there was a way to support David while still fulfilling her own responsibilities. But that wasn't the way the world worked.

"Is someone going to get that?" Miriam's voice yelled from somewhere across the building. Amanda's view was blocked by the pasteurization equipment. All she could see was her own distorted reflection in the shiny metal vats.

The phone rang again. "*Ya. Oll recht.* I'll get it." Amanda sighed, braced herself and picked up the receiver. "Hello?"

"Amanda?"

Her heart did a flip-flop at the sound of the voice on the other end of the line. "David?"

"*Ya.* It's me."

"I didn't expect to hear from you."

"*Nee*, I guess not." She heard him exhale. "I'm sorry to call. You made yourself clear yesterday. I want to respect that but…" The call fell silent except for the quiet rasp of his breath.

"David, what's happened? I don't like the sound of your voice."

"I'm sorry, Amanda. I need help. I know I shouldn't ask. I took your contract and I know you want it back.

The truth is, you could get it back if you don't help me right now. And I wouldn't blame you. But I have to ask."

Amanda shook her head, even though he couldn't see the motion. "David, slow down. What's going on?"

"The mohair I need for the contract is ruined unless I figure out how to salvage it."

"All of it?"

"Pretty much."

Amanda pulled out the rolling desk chair from beneath the Formica countertop and sat down hard. "Tell me what's going on."

She could hardly believe the story as David recounted the events of that morning.

"The skunk sprayed the entire herd? Directly?"

"They were all penned together in preparation for the shearing. I thought I was doing everything right."

"You were. How could you know that a skunk would get in?"

"Have you ever heard of something like this before?"

"I've heard of skunks and goats having run-ins before, but nothing this disastrous."

"Amanda, if I can't get the smell out of that mohair, I'm finished. I know I shouldn't ask, but can you help me? Do you know what to do?"

Amanda bit her lip. This was her chance to get the contract back. If David couldn't fulfill it, there was an excellent chance she could convince the company to give it back to her. But the thought was not even tempting. Sure, she wanted that contract back, but not like this.

"I'm on my way." Amanda hung up the phone and stood up. There was only one thing to do and, in her heart, she knew it was right.

Amanda's hired *Englisch* driver pulled up to David's farmhouse soon after. The pungent odor of skunk met her as soon as she flung open the car door. She wrinkled her nose and slammed the door. David and his family were across the farmyard with the goats, their faces taut. She could feel the tension, even from a distance. He was crouched down, cradling a nanny in his arms with a bucket of water beside him. His attention jerked to Amanda and he hurried out of the goat pen.

"You came," he said as soon as she was in earshot.

"I said I was on my way."

"*Ya*, but it seemed too *gut* to be true."

Gravel crunched as the *Englisch* driver backed up and turned around in the driveway. A tractor engine hummed somewhere in the distance. "So, I'm too good to be true now, am I?" Amanda flashed a shy smile. She hoped that teasing him might lift the mood.

David shook his head, but returned the smile, even though his eyes stayed sad. "Only you could make me feel better at a time like this."

"You're not answering my question, you know."

David chuckled. Then his expression turned serious as he looked into her eyes. "You know you are, Amanda." He moved his hand to her arm and gently squeezed. "*Danki* for coming."

Amanda's stomach fluttered. His hand felt so warm and comforting through the thin cotton of her blue cape dress. And his expression was so sincere. He was grateful that she was here. He valued her. Seeing that true appreciation almost made it worth losing the contract to him. "You know I had to *kumme*."

"*Nee*, you didn't. My loss would be your gain. If you didn't help me, you could win that contract back."

"Some things are more important than business."

"Like me?" Now it was David's turn to flash a teasing smile. And this time, his eyes were not quite as sad.

Amanda wanted to say yes, he was. Because she loved him. And that was worth more than any contract. She wanted him to succeed. She wanted him to be happy. She could not take that from him, even if it cost her. But she could not tell him that, so she said nothing. And she wasn't sure if he wanted to hear the truth. He might just be flirting in order to break the tension. It might mean nothing.

David waited for her to answer. When she didn't, he cleared his throat and looked down.

"We better get started," Amanda said.

"Right. Of course."

"What have you done so far?"

"I've been checking their eyes, making sure there's no irritation from a direct spray. A couple nanny goats needed to have their eyes flushed. I've taken care of that."

"*Gut*. That's exactly what I would have done first."

David nodded.

"I don't know if we can save any fiber that took a direct hit, but we can try," Amanda said.

"Maybe the rest of it."

"Let's hope so."

"So, what do you think would work best?" David asked.

Amanda tapped a finger against her chin as she studied the goats. They milled about the pen, bleating occasionally and butting the fence post. "They look unhappy."

"I'm sure they are. It's been a bad experience for them."

"Poor things," Amanda murmured as she thought through the options. "We can't use tomato juice. It would stain the fiber."

"*Ya*. I've heard some people say that doesn't work, anyway."

Amanda nodded. "Best thing I know to do is to wash them in a solution of hydrogen peroxide, baking soda and liquid dish soap. That's the safest option."

Soon, David's mother was hurrying to round up the ingredients from the pantry. She stopped on her way to put a hand on Amanda's shoulder. "*Danki*," she said, eyes serious. "It was *gut* for you to *kumme* and help. We needed it." She glanced over at her son, then back to Amanda. "David tells me you're the expert."

Amanda would have beamed over the compliment a few hours ago, but now she was too afraid of letting the family down. "I just hope my idea works. I've read that it's the best thing to take the smell of skunk out of any kind of fiber." Amanda shook her head. "But I can't make any promises."

Lydia gave a gentle smile. "All we can do is our best, ain't so?" And then she was off, scurrying toward the farmhouse without waiting for an answer. Not long after that, the entire family, plus Amanda, were hunkered down with the goats, scrubbing and scouring. Amanda wrinkled her nose as she splashed a goat with clean water to wash away the soap.

"Here," Lloyd said and handed Amanda a strip of white cloth. "Try this. Lydia tore up an old sheet. It helps. Well, a little, at least."

"*Danki.*" Amanda tied the strip of cloth around her face to cover her nose and mouth, then splashed another bucket of clean water over the goat. The animal shivered, then bleated. "I know, I know," Amanda said as she patted the goat's flank. "None of this is any fun."

They washed each goat, one after another, until they had worked through the entire herd. David shook his head and wiped his forehead with the back of his hand. "It's no *gut*. We have to do another round."

After scrubbing and rinsing each goat a second time, Amanda sat down on an overturned feed bucket and sighed. Her knees ached from crouching in the mud and her nostrils burned from the smell of skunk.

"It still smells bad," Katie said. She wrinkled her nose and looked up at David.

"She's right," David said. "It's better, but the smell is still there. Maybe if I had more time, but they want the fiber delivered by the end of the week. There's no way it's going to be okay by then."

Lydia patted a goat, then straightened up. "It's not so bad," she said.

"Not so bad isn't *gut* enough," David said.

Lydia exhaled. "I know."

They all waited in silence for a moment. Amanda knew that no one could bear to give up. Finally, Lloyd dropped his wash rag into one of the buckets and said, "*Vell*, that's that, I guess."

"*Ya.*" David looked older than he had the day before. There were lines on his face that had not been there earlier. "I guess so."

But no one moved. They just sat or stood, staring at the goats and the loss of the family's livelihood.

* * *

David could not believe it was over. All his dreams and hopes dashed. There was no fixing this, no last-minute reprieve. He would lose the farm. It was almost too much to bear, especially when he had been so close to saving it. This contract had been the miracle he had been praying for. Or so he had thought.

His parents and sister trudged toward the farmhouse to get cleaned up and he found himself alone with Amanda. The sun was setting and long, golden rays poured across the goat pen, lighting the white fleeces with warm halos. It would have been beautiful, if it had not been so ironic. All that good, rich fiber, ruined.

Behind the goat pen, the sky blushed pink above the rolling hills and pastureland. A hawk soared high above, silhouetted against a silver-lined cloud. David could not appreciate the beauty, because soon he would not be looking at the sky from his place in the farmyard. He would not look out and see the cornfields and pear orchard beyond his property line. He would not see the children playing in the yard of the one-room schoolhouse at the end of the road. He would not see his mother's face light up when she placed a casserole dish on the kitchen table and they all sat down together, in their own house.

"I've lost everything," he said.

Amanda turned her face up to look at him. "It's a loss, but there'll be other contracts, other chances. You'll lose this shearing, but in six months, you'll get another one."

David took off his straw hat and turned it slowly in his hands. "*Nee.* There won't be another chance." Shame tiptoed up his spine to heat his face. "I haven't been able to admit the whole truth to you. This was my last chance.

The farm has lost too much money and I can't get any more credit. It's over. Without the money from this contract, I have to sell up, move back to an apartment in town and go back to the factory."

Amanda's lips parted, but no words came out. Her forehead creased. She stayed like that for a few beats before closing her mouth and shaking her head. "I don't know what to say."

"Because there's nothing to say. There's nothing that anyone can do now."

"I knew you wanted that contract, but I didn't understand how vital it was. I'm sorry. I should have realized. I should have…" Amanda frowned and looked away, toward the horizon. "I can't think of anything worse than losing my farm."

"Then you understand." David managed a weak smile. "At least I'm not alone in that."

They sat in silence for a long time. David could sense Amanda's empathy for him. That was the only thing that kept him from complete collapse. A small flicker of warmth stayed alive inside his chest, a weak but very real flame against the darkness. She had set aside what was in her own best interest to help him. She had ended their rivalry and tried to save him.

"It means a lot to me that you came to help," David said. He turned to look at her. She was staring at the last glow of sunset. He studied her profile as shadows overtook the farmyard.

"It didn't make a difference." She did not turn to look at him. Her eyes stayed on the horizon. "I'm sorry."

David exhaled and gathered the courage to tell her the truth. "It did make a difference."

Amanda's gaze swung to him. Her brow furrowed. "How?"

"Because I know that you care."

"Oh." She swallowed. Her eyes stayed on his, her expression unreadable.

David's pulse pounded in his temples. He needed her to respond.

"It was the right thing to do. We're Amish. Sometimes I act more like an *Englischer*," she said. She turned her gaze back to the horizon. "I'm too competitive. I know that. I want everyone to see that I'm *gut* at what I do. It's *hochmut*."

David's stomach twisted. He wanted Amanda to say that she had come because she loved him. Was she only here out of duty? That was a good thing and it showed her commitment to the faith, but he couldn't help feeling a stab of disappointment. "I've been prideful too." Maybe if he opened up more, she would as well. Besides, it was true and he needed to confess it to her.

A faint smile tugged at Amanda's lips. "Now's the time for me to tease you for your *hochmut* when we first met. You were so prideful at the livestock auction and the Feed & Seed." But it was clear she did not feel like joking with him. Her smile was thoughtful and sad.

"*Ya*. Same as you," David said. His voice was as wistful as her smile.

"We both had a lot to prove," Amanda said.

"I had too much pride to admit that my farm was failing. I couldn't even tell you the truth in my letters."

"I wouldn't have been as hard on you if I'd known."

"You sure about that?"

Amanda chuckled softly, then sighed. "I really am sorry, David."

"I know. And I appreciate it. I thought you might gloat when you heard."

Amanda's attention jerked to him, her brown eyes boring into his. He could see the hurt in them. "You really thought that about me? I was prideful, but I was never cruel. Don't you know my heart better than that?"

"*Ya.* I knew better. But I was still afraid."

Amanda nodded slowly. "I was afraid too."

"Amanda Stoltzfus, afraid?" David smiled. "I'm not sure I believe it."

"I thought you knew me better than that by now."

"I'd like to. You can be hard to read."

"I'm not very complicated," Amanda said.

"*Nee*, I guess not." David plucked a blade of grass and twisted it between his fingers. "Maybe I'm just not *gut* at reading people."

"Or maybe I'm pretty *gut* at putting up walls."

"Maybe we both are."

Darkness crept over the farmyard, like a purple blanket pulled over a bed. The sun was gone, the faint glow above the horizon lost to night. David wanted to say so much more to Amanda, but the moment felt too fragile. He didn't want to mess up the connection they had made today. And, after all he had been through over the last few hours, he did not trust himself to say the right thing. He was too wrung out with emotions. He wanted to tell her that he loved her. He wanted to tell her that he would never be the same now that she was in his life. He wanted to tell her that the loss of his farm wasn't as bad, knowing that he might have a future with her. But he was afraid to count on that future. They had never spoken of it and she might not feel the same. "Will you stay for supper?" he said instead. It was the best he could do.

Amanda took a deep breath and let it out. "I can't. Leah, John and both the *bopplin* have come down with colds. They'll need me to help with the milking. We have a big family, but sometimes there still aren't enough hands to go around. Not with two fussy *bopplin* who always need holding."

"You've got a big farm. It's a lot to keep up with."

Amanda's face tensed. "I'm sorry. I didn't mean to…" She shook her head. "I shouldn't have brought up my farm."

"It's *oll recht*. You're just telling me about your life. Life still goes on, even when things fall apart."

"I wish I could fix this for you, David."

"You can't fix everything, Amanda. Time to let it go. It isn't your responsibility. I'll drive you home now. It's the least I can do after all your help." He exhaled, then added, "I'll always appreciate what you did here today."

Amanda stood up from where she had been sitting on the overturned feed bucket. "*Nee*, there's no need for you to bother. Go get cleaned up. It's a long drive and I know it's been a long day." She stretched her back, then hesitated before walking away. "Goodbye, David." Her eyes met his and stayed there a few beats longer than expected.

"It's not goodbye yet. I'm walking you to the phone shanty and waiting with you until your driver gets here if you won't let me take you myself."

She gave a faint smile. "If you insist."

"I do." He would savor the time they had left together

today. Without farming to unite them, what would keep their friendship going? David wondered if Amanda would be interested in him when he went back to being a factory worker. It was good, honest work, but what would they talk about? She had no interest in it. Neither did he. But he would have to find a way to make the most of it. All he had to get him through now was his faith, even if it felt like *Gott* had abandoned him. He would fight to keep believing.

And part of that fight was recognizing that Amanda had come to help him today. She did care. Her feelings for him had superseded her own interests. That meant a lot. Now he had to decide what to do about it. He had lost his farm today, but had he gained Amanda?

Chapter Eleven

The next day, Amanda was leaving the goat shed after the evening milking when she saw Miriam striding toward her with a tight, unreadable expression.

"Is everything *oll recht*?" Amanda asked.

"I just got a strange phone call on the business line."

Amanda frowned. "From who?"

"Lancaster Fleece & Fiber. They wanted to talk to you, so I took a message."

"They wanted to talk to me?" Amanda asked.

"*Ya.* That's what I just said."

"Did—"

"Amanda, what is happening with that contract?" Miriam interrupted. "They made it sound like we lost it. But then, apparently, we didn't after all? None of it made sense and I didn't want to ask them. Our family would look incompetent. So, I just went along with it. You've got some explaining to do."

Amanda exhaled. "I just learned about it on Sunday."

"Learned what?" Miriam set her hands on her hips and waited.

"They aren't renewing the contract. They took it from us and gave it to someone else."

"How did you find out on a Sunday? You shouldn't have been checking messages or doing any kind of business on the Sabbath."

"I wasn't. They weren't the ones who told me. The truth is, I've been avoiding them. I couldn't face listening to their voicemail. I'm sorry I—"

Miriam held up her hand. "So how did you find out?"

"Because they gave it to David Troyer."

"Your secret pen pal?"

"If that's what you want to call him."

"It's accurate, ain't so?"

"*Was* accurate."

Miriam studied Amanda's expression for a moment. "You *oll recht*?"

"*Ya.*" Amanda looked away. She was feeling too much all at once to explain. A few days ago, losing that contract had felt like the worst thing possible. Now all she could think about was David's loss and how she would rather he have the contract instead of her. The realization rattled her and she stood without speaking for a moment.

"Amanda?"

Amanda jerked her attention back to Miriam.

"You don't look okay."

"I am."

"You sure?"

"Of course."

Miriam sighed but did not argue. "So, he told you about it when you went visiting?"

"*Ya.* He had no idea it had been our contract and that it was up for renewal and that we were in negotiations for it."

"You should have told me."

"I was going to. I just needed some time." Amanda squeezed her eyes shut. "I feel like the biggest failure in the world. This is the one thing I do well, and I lost our most important contract."

"*Vell*, that's the confusing part. I don't think we did lose it."

Amanda's eyes flew open. "What?"

"I told you the call didn't make sense."

"What exactly did they say?"

"That you need to call them back right away. They want to give you a second chance at renewing it."

Amanda stiffened. "They what?"

Miriam smiled. "You heard me. Looks like it might not be over, after all."

Amanda tried to make sense of what she had just heard.

Miriam shooed her toward the production building. "You better call them back, ain't so?"

"*Recht.*" She turned abruptly, stumbled, caught her balance, then hitched up her skirt and sprinted.

Amanda's hand was shaking as she dialed the number that Miriam had written down on a notepad beside the telephone. She pulled out the rolling desk chair and started to sit down, then popped up again. She was too nervous to stay still. The phone rang once, twice. Amanda twisted the cord around a finger as she paced as far as it reached, then turned and paced the opposite direction. The phone rang again. Amanda wondered if she was too late. It was after business hours. Had they really meant for her to call today?

But on the fourth ring, someone picked up. There was static in the background, followed by a shuffling sound and muffled voices. Then a voice spoke up clearly. "Terry Baker here."

"Hello, this is Amanda Stoltzfus. I got the message to call you?"

"Yes, thanks for getting back to me so quickly. I'm at the grocery store with my kids, so I'm going to be quick." She laughed. "They're not going to give us much time."

Amanda chuckled politely, but did not smile.

"Look," Terry said. "We had decided to give the contract to another producer. We wanted to go in a different direction."

Amanda wrapped the cord more tightly around her finger. "You gave it to David Troyer, right?"

There was a slight pause. "Yes. How did you know?"

"It's a small world, I guess."

"Mmm. Sounds like it. Especially since David pointed me back in your direction."

"He did?"

"Hold on." Amanda heard a muffled voice in the background. A few beats passed. "Okay, I'm back. What were we saying?"

"David Troyer—"

"Right. He's not going to be able to fulfill the contract after all. So, he told us to talk to you. He really went to bat for you." She laughed. "And we were ready to listen. The truth is, we've been left in the lurch here. We've got our own orders to fulfill with our buyers. It would be a favor to us if you'd sign a contract right away. I think you'll find the offer is generous enough to persuade you to keep working with us. Let me just pull those numbers up." After a brief pause, Terry read out the figures. "Does that work for you?"

Amanda blinked a few times. "It certain sure does. That's a very *gut* offer." She could hardly believe it.

"Great. I'll send over the contract for you to sign as soon as I get back to the office tomorrow morning."

"Great," Amanda said right before the line went dead. She stood in silence for a moment, then sat down hard in the desk chair. What had just happened? David had thought about her, that was what. He wanted her to be happy. He wanted what was best for her. Right now, during one of the darkest days of his life, he was thinking of her. He didn't have to refer Lancaster Fleece & Fiber to her. He didn't have to tell them that she was ready and willing to take the same contract. But he had. He cared about her. And he believed in her.

This should have been a delicious moment of victory. She had the contract again that she had needed so badly. But all she could think about was what David had lost. Something strange and wonderful was happening. She didn't care as much about succeeding as she did about David. She didn't need to carry the weight of her family's farm entirely on her shoulders. They would manage, even if she wasn't perfect. She didn't have to prove herself anymore. Suddenly, she felt light and free. Nothing mattered as much as standing with him. It might mean losing some of what she had just gained, but she would find a way to make it work. She always did.

Now she had to do the right thing. And fast.

David was putting his supper dish in the sink when headlights shined through the kitchen window and lit up the room. Gravel crunched in the driveway, followed by the slam of a car door and fast-moving footsteps. His heart leaped into his throat. Could it be Amanda? Had she heard what he had done? Was she angry? Or happy? He squinted against the light, but couldn't make out the car or driver in the glare.

There was a hard knock on the door followed by a pause, then another knock. He sprinted to open it and found Amanda staring up at him, her cheeks flushed red and a strand of hair fallen lose from her *kapp*. "I'm sorry it's late. I had to talk to you."

David swallowed hard. "They called you about the contract?"

"*Ya*." Amanda shook her head. Her brow furrowed and David was afraid that she was going to tell him that he should have stayed out of her affairs. He knew how much she valued her independence. She needed to prove to everyone that she could succeed on her own. "I don't know what to say." She shook her head again, harder this time, and her *kapp* strings slapped her cheeks. "You made sure they went back to me with the contract."

"Are you surprised?"

The furrow in Amanda's brow deepened. "*Nee*. It's exactly the kind of thing you would do. I see that now."

"And you're…upset?"

"Upset?" Amanda laughed and the wrinkle in her brow smoothed out. "I came to thank you. I'm not upset, I'm…touched."

"Oh," David said. He wanted to say so much more, but he couldn't. He was too transfixed by the look in Amanda's eyes. She was gazing up at him with what looked like love. Or he hoped it was. "It was the least I could do."

"After I told you that I had to try to take the contract back, you could have been spiteful and made sure I didn't get it. Or at the very least, you could have just not said anything. Instead, you convinced them to give it to me."

"I hope I didn't overstep."

Amanda's lips turned up in a faint smile. "Maybe I would have thought so a few days ago. But now, I realize..." She looked down at her hands. "That you have a *gut* heart. I guess I always knew that, ever since we started writing to each other. But after we met..."

"I'm glad I could help," David said.

"I know."

"*Kumme* in from the cold. I'll put the kettle on and warm you up with some tea."

Amanda rubbed her arms. "I didn't realize it was cold. But I feel it now. I guess I was too excited before." She glanced behind her. "I shouldn't let my hired driver go. I should have him take me home now."

"You came all the way here, just to turn around? I think we can make a better plan."

"*Vell*, there is more that I wanted to say to you." Amanda rubbed her arms again.

"Tell you what, let's take that tea to go," David said. "I'll drive you back in the buggy. That'll give us plenty of time to talk."

Amanda blinked. "You want to drive me home?"

Was he being too forward? Men only drove women home when they were courting. Of course, that was when they were going home from church or youth group meetings. This was different. They had both been through a lot of emotions over the last few days. They both needed to talk. Did that make it reasonable?

Of course, if she *did* think that he wanted to court, and she was agreeable to it, that would be ideal. But he didn't want to risk rejection. Not now. Not after all he had just lost.

"You don't mind?" Amanda's forehead crinkled as she studied his face.

David hooked his thumbs beneath his suspenders. "Best to get out and think of other things, *ya*?"

"*Ya.*" Amanda glanced back at the hired driver. "If you're sure you don't mind."

"Tell him to go on. I'll hitch up the buggy."

"*Oll recht.* I'd like that." When she looked up at David, her eyes were shining. Maybe his life wasn't completely falling apart, after all.

Soon, they were both in the buggy, rumbling down the gravel driveway. Amanda's hands were wrapped around a mug of tea and her face was upturned, toward the sky. The stars were out and they shined overhead like a basket of diamonds spilled across black velvet. The horse snorted and tugged at the reins as the wheels clattered onto the pavement.

"It's a pretty night," David said. Suddenly, he couldn't think of anything to say but the obvious. He felt like they were teenagers courting for the first time. But, of course, they weren't courting. Were they? She had never agreed to anything. But how much was implied? Some folks would say this meant they were courting automatically. But Amanda didn't seem to go by what other folks said.

"*Ya,*" Amanda murmured. "It's nice out."

David was painfully aware of how close Amanda was. He could feel the warmth of her arm brushing against his and hear the quiet rasp of her breath. He wanted to move both of the reins over to his left hand and slip his right arm around her shoulder. He wondered if he dared.

"I have a proposal for you," Amanda said.

"Oh?" He was glad that he had not tried to hold her. "A business proposal, you mean?" Or did she mean something more personal? She was bold, but surely she wouldn't be the one to suggest that they court. That was unheard-of among the Amish. He wouldn't mind if she did, though. It would be a huge relief, actually.

Amanda hesitated. "*Ya.* A business proposal."

"*Oll recht.*" David's heart sank a little, but he made sure not to show it. "What is it?"

"I can't take that contract from you. It isn't right."

"You seemed okay with trying to take it away from me on Sunday, remember?"

Amanda puffed up her cheeks, then blew out the air. "Things are different now."

David grunted. "Things change that fast?"

"I think they've been changing for a while."

"Fair enough."

"And when I told you I had to fight for the contract, I meant a fair fight. Not..." Amanda made a waving motion with her hand. "Not taking it back because something bad happened to your herd."

David nodded. "It was a tough blow, for certain sure."

"Maybe it doesn't have to be."

David took his attention off the road long enough to glance over at her. Her eyes were clear and bright.

"I've been thinking." She straightened in her seat and gripped her mug more tightly. "There's a way for you to keep the contract and save the farm."

David's heart skipped a beat. "How?"

"*Vell*, it's pretty obvious, ain't so?"

David shook his head. "Is it?"

Amanda smiled, but her jaw looked tight. David could tell that she was nervous and excited, both at the same time. His pulse sped up in anticipation.

"We join forces. If we combine our herds, then you don't lose the contract."

David sat still for a moment. He watched the buggy horse trotting in front of them, her mane rippling in the wind. Was Amanda saying what he thought she was saying? "That would mean joining our businesses." He said the words slowly and tentatively, then snuck a sideways glance at her.

Amanda swallowed hard and looked down. "*Ya.* It would."

David was afraid to say what he hoped she was hinting at. Was her business proposal a marriage proposal in disguise? That would be the best possible news. He could be with the woman he loved and keep farming. It was too good to be true. But, as his mother often said, if it sounds too good to be true, it probably is. "So, this would be a business arrangement?"

Amanda hesitated. "Of course."

David shifted in his seat. It did not sound like there was any hidden romantic motive behind the suggestion. But he needed to be sure. Except that it would be too humiliating to ask directly, then find out that she was doing this out of charity alone. He would appreciate the gesture—it was selfless and kind—but his heart could not take the rejection. Not today. He had to tread carefully. "You sure your siblings would be okay with that? You could lose money, not to mention control. I'd be a part of a family business."

Amanda frowned. "Miriam wouldn't agree unless…"

Amanda bit her lip, glanced at David, then back at the dark road ahead. Pine trees lined the way, the needles rustling in the night breeze. "*Vell*, don't take this the wrong way, but you'd have to join the family to be part of the family business. Miriam would never risk losing control of our interests."

David tugged the reins, and the buggy shuddered to a stop, right there on the highway. There was no traffic and no noise, just the sound of Amanda's breath and the swish of the horse's tail. Was he understanding correctly? Could it really be true? "Amanda, are you suggesting that we get married?"

"*Ach, nee.* Or technically, yes. I mean… It's a business arrangement."

David stared into her eyes, trying to decipher her motivation. "So, it's just business?"

Amanda gave a quick nod. "*Ya.* Just…business."

David's stomach dropped. For a moment there, he thought maybe she wanted something more. Something real. But that had been foolish of him. He was a failure. A woman like Amanda would never want to marry a man like him for romantic reasons. She was just being a *gut*, selfless friend. Which only made him love her more. She had transformed over the last few days. When they first met, she would never have made such a sacrificial offer. But now, she was willing to tie herself to him for life out of concern for his welfare? It was extraordinary. There must be more to it.

David turned back to the road and slapped the reins. The horse snorted, shook her mane and took off in a trot. The buggy jerked forward and they were moving again.

"I see how this benefits me. But what's in it for you?" It was time to be a bit blunt.

"It meant a lot to me when I found out that you tried to get Lancaster Fleece & Fiber to give me back the contract. I felt…" She pursed her lips and looked away. "I don't know. I thought it would be the right thing to do. I wanted to help you."

"How can I accept that kind of charity? You'd be stuck with me for the rest of your life."

"It would benefit me too. You've got a *gut* herd and I've been wanting to increase our fiber production. We're primarily a dairy farm, while you're primarily a fiber farm. It makes sense. I thought it would help us both."

David tightened his grip on the reins. He wanted so badly to say yes. He wanted to spend the rest of his life with Amanda. He wanted to trek up the hill behind her farmhouse every evening and watch the stars come out. He wanted to sit by the fire with her on cold winter nights. He wanted to wake up before the sun with her and milk the goats side by side while laughing and teasing one another. It would be a good life. A life he had always wanted.

But it would not be real. It would be a fake marriage, one of convenience. She did not love him, not in that way. Sure, there had been that almost-kiss. But marriage? That was an entirely different thing altogether. An almost-kiss did not mean that she was in love with him. And besides, he might have misinterpreted that moment altogether. He probably had. Otherwise, she would have told him the truth when he asked her what kind of marriage this would be. Amanda was bold and forthright. She would not pretend to want a marriage of convenience if she wanted a love match. She would tell him outright. He had asked, and she had answered. He had to accept reality. And he had to answer in the only way he could.

David knew that he could not accept an act of charity this enormous. He would not ask her to sacrifice her future for him. She still had a chance to find a husband she would love. He would not take that from her. He loved her too much.

Chapter Twelve

Amanda's heart pounded in her throat. She could not take it. What would he say? She had put everything on the line: her pride, her hopes, her future. It was a wild thing to do. What kind of Amish woman proposed to a man? One like her, apparently. She had never held to conventions and now was not the time to start.

Amanda's eyes flicked up to study David's expression, then darted away again before he could return her gaze. For a wonderful, glorious moment, she had thought that he would say yes. She had been sure of her plan, but now she was flooded with doubt. It had all gone wrong when he asked outright if she was proposing to him. That had been her chance to tell the truth. She had panicked instead.

Amanda had finally found a man who respected her for who she was, who appreciated her talents and interests. Who made her heart race at the sound of his voice, or at the warm touch of his hand in hers. Yes, she was asking him to marry her. And not as a business arrangement.

But how could she admit that to him? Sure, she felt certain that he had fallen for her too. He had almost said as much. But a marriage proposal was going way too far. Even if he was in love with her, it didn't mean that he wanted to marry her. He might want a conventional wife who would focus on the hearth and home, not on raising goats and turning a profit. That didn't sound like him, but it was a possibility. Or he might be offended that she would be so bold. Amish women didn't signal their interest to men. They waited to be courted. They did not initiate the courting. And they certainly did not initiate a marriage proposal!

So, when he had asked her outright what she wanted, Amanda had made an excuse. Now she waited for him to tell her that he didn't want it to be a business arrangement, that he wanted it to be a real marriage.

But he said nothing.

She desperately wondered what he was thinking. His jaw looked tight, his shoulders hunched forward, his brow deeply furrowed. He did not look happy. He looked embarrassed, angry even. Had she hurt his pride? As Amish, neither of them was supposed to give in to that emotion, but in reality, she knew it was a great weakness for both of them.

Amanda bounced in her seat as the buggy rattled over a pothole. She braced herself against the dashboard and tried to force her heart to slow down. But she could not bear the waiting any longer. "David?" she said at last. He had to give her an answer. Her heart was pounding against her ribs. Her palms were sweaty and her mouth was dry. She felt like she might pass out.

He shifted the reins to one hand, rubbed his eyes with a thumb and forefinger, then moved the reins back to both hands. He let out a long, slow breath. "I appreciate what you're offering. But you know that I can't accept."

Amanda's stomach dropped. She felt as if her heart sank all the way down to the pavement, as if the buggy rolled right over it and left it flattened behind her. She would keep going, but her heart would stay there on the road, battered and broken. This was the last rejection she would ever allow. This one was the most humiliating, the most unbearable. The only one that came from a man she loved.

"Amanda?" David's voice was soft and gentle. He was being kind, even as he rejected her. That was how good a man he was. He didn't want to hurt her. It only made her love him more.

"*Ya.*" She shook herself free of the pain. She would shut it down, like she always had. Hadn't she survived other rejections? Of course she had. She would survive this one too. Her heart shouted otherwise, but her brain insisted that she could get over this. She was strong. She knew how to swallow her hurt and keep going. She had already given up on love long ago.

A rush of emotion swelled within her. It was that restored hope that made this so painful. After all those rejections, all that humiliation, she had finally found someone who loved her. Or so she had thought.

Amanda fought the surge of emotion. "I understand. It was a *narrisch* idea." Her mind raced for an excuse. "I just wanted to give back to a friend. I couldn't bear to see you lose everything."

David nodded slowly. "That's what I thought." He smiled softly. "It wasn't ridiculous. But it's not realistic, either." He turned, and the kindness on his face nearly broke her. "It was a very thoughtful thing to do. But you understand why I can't accept."

"Of course." Amanda understood perfectly. He did not want to spend his life chained to her, even if it saved his livelihood. She looked out over the darkened fields. They passed a white farmhouse with windows that glowed yellow from the flickering light of a propane lamp. She imagined a family in there together, the husband and wife tucking the children in bed, then settling by the woodstove for a cup of hot chocolate while they chatted about their day. That was the life that she had wanted with David. The life that she would never have.

David's heart ached so deeply that he could feel it as a physical pain. Saying no to Amanda's offer hurt even worse than the heartbreak of losing his farm. As much as his farm meant to him, it was not as important as the woman he loved. Nothing could mean as much to him as the people he loved. And now he had failed nearly all of them. His family would have to give up their happy days on their own land, in their cozy little farmhouse, to cram back into a cheap apartment in town. At least he wasn't letting Amanda down. She must have been relieved to hear that he would not take her up on her offer. When she woke up in the morning, she would shake off the idea and realize what a rash, unreasonable thing she had suggested. She would be thankful to still be free.

When he woke up the next day, on the other hand, there was no relief, only the grim acceptance that he had done the right thing. Even so, as he settled into his chair at the kitchen table, there was a nagging feeling that he should have said more. He had been a coward. But what would have been the point of telling her outright that he wished for a real marriage? It was best to spare himself the humiliation and her the awkwardness.

"I made your favorite," Lydia said as she slid a fat slice of Amish breakfast casserole onto his plate.

"*Danki*." David picked up his fork. The egg, cheese, sausage and bacon dish smelled delicious, but he didn't have an appetite. He let his fork hover over his plate as he stared at his food.

"I know it's a tough time, but you have to keep your strength up," Lydia said. "Try to eat a little."

David nodded and took a bite. It did taste wonderful good, but he could barely manage to force it down.

Lloyd walked by, a copy of *The Budget* newspaper tucked under one arm, and patted David on the shoulder. "We've been through tough times before. We'll get through this one too, with *Gott*'s help."

Lydia slid into her chair and smiled. "And there might just be a silver lining to this. It brought you and Amanda together, ain't so? She's a treasure, David—rushing over here to try and save the herd. But I guess you already know that."

David sighed. "*Ya*. I know that for certain sure."

Katie appeared in the doorway, rubbing her eyes and yawning. "Can we take the goats with us when we leave the farm?"

David and his mother exchanged glances.

"You explained the situation to her?" David asked in a low voice.

Lydia nodded. "Better to let her know now so she has time to adjust."

"She loves it here," David murmured.

Lydia reached across the table to pat David's arm. "It's okay."

"*Mamm*, you and David are whispering instead of answering my question. I'm right here, so I know you're talking about me." She folded her arms and stared them both down. "Why do grown-ups always have to keep secrets?"

"We're not keeping secrets," David said. But even as he spoke the words, he felt a tug at his conscience. He was keeping a secret. He had not told Amanda how he really felt. He had let her go without communicating his true feelings. But that was best, wasn't it? He was protecting them both from a messy, hurtful reality... Right?

"Goats need to live outside, where they can forage and play," Lydia said gently. "They can't live in an apartment."

Katie's face fell. "Oh." She scrunched up her mouth and David could see that she was trying not to cry. It was more than he could take. He pushed his plate away from him and stood up so fast that his chair toppled over behind him with a crash.

"Sorry," he said as he hurried to set it upright again. "I, uh, just need to check on the herd and get the milking done. There's still work to do as long as we're still here."

"Won't you try to eat a little more?" Lydia asked. Her eyes searched his. She looked older than she had the day before, which only added to his despair.

"*Nee*. I'm sorry. I know you made it for me. I'll reheat some later."

He had never pulled on his work boots so quickly. Before anyone could say another word, he was out the door, breathing in the fresh morning air. The cold burned his lungs, but he didn't care. It felt good to breathe his own air on his own land, while he still could. He noticed the sun peeking above the horizon and watched as it bathed the farmyard in a golden glow. The chickens pecked at the earth and the goats bleated in the pen. A red wagon stacked with feed waited beside the goat shed. Everything seemed right and good, but that was an illusion.

David tried not to think. He just needed to go through the motions of the day. Better not to analyze or feel. He could only take so much. The one thing that gave him peace was that he had done the right thing to protect Amanda from a future that she did not want. At least he had not used her to save his farm. That would have been inexcusable. When he signed the property over to someone else, he would have that to comfort him.

David unlatched the gate and let himself into the main goat pen. The stench of skunk sill lingered, but it was more bearable today. "Hello, friends," he murmured as he stopped to pet a nanny on the head, then scratch behind another's ears. A goat butted him gently and he laughed. "All right, I won't leave you out, girl." He knelt down to scratch behind her ears too. As he did, he noticed a little white goat in the corner of the pen that he had never seen before. "And who are you, little one?"

His heart warmed when he realized that one of the nannies had given birth in the night. The kid pressed against his mother's side while he gazed at David with expressive black eyes. The world must seem fresh and new when viewed through those eyes, David thought. Full of hope and promises. Full of excitement at what might come.

David watched as the kid ventured toward him on

shaky legs. "Hello there," David murmured as he reached out to pet him. "Welcome to the world."

When David dropped his hand, the kid bleated and pushed against David's leg. David chuckled and scratched behind the little goat's ears. His coat felt soft as silk beneath his fingers.

As David knelt in the goat pen, amid all that he had lost, the curious, eager kid had a strange effect on him. He watched the spark of new life dancing behind the kid's eyes, saw it struggle to stay up on wobbly knees, and David knew that he could not quit now. There was too much to hope for, too much to experience.

He had given up too soon.

This tiny, fragile kid had not given up, and neither had its mother. She had brought forth new life in the still dark of night, when hope felt the most impossible.

David knew what he had to do. He had to be brave. He had to reveal the truth—the full truth—to Amanda. Then she could make up her own mind about what to do. By withholding how he felt, he had robbed her of the autonomy to make her own decision. And he had robbed himself of a chance at true happiness. She might back out when she learned that he wanted more than a business arrangement. He might be humiliated. But he might not. And the chance to marry Amanda for the right reasons was worth the risk.

David did not take the time to hitch up the buggy and crawl across the county at a horse's pace. He did what Amanda had done when there was an urgent situation and called his *Englisch* driver. He ran the entire way to the phone shanty and back. Then, as he waited for the driver to arrive, he switched from his straw hat to his

Sunday-best black felt hat. This was a special occasion and he ought to look the part.

By the time the hired car roared into Amanda's driveway in a cloud of dust, David could barely contain himself. His palms were sweating and his pulse was hammering in his temples. But he was sure that this was the right thing—the only thing—to do.

The screen door banged open and shut and Naomi appeared on the front porch wearing a gray work kerchief and a stained apron. Belinda honked and waddled toward the car. Ollie barked and wagged his tail.

David leaped out of the car, stumbling when his feet hit the loose gravel. "I've got to talk to Amanda," he shouted.

"She's not here."

David's stomach plummeted. He could not wait another minute. He had to tell Amanda now, before he lost his nerve. And before he tormented himself wondering what her reaction would be. "Do you know where I can find her?"

"Um, I think she went into Bluebird Hills' downtown. She had some errands to run."

"*Danki!*" David shouted as he dived back into the car. When they arrived on Mainstreet, David told the driver to go to the end of the block. He figured he knew exactly where Amanda would be. David grinned when he saw that he was right. Clyde was tied to the hitching post outside of the Bluebird Hills Feed & Seed, swishing his tail and munching on oats.

"You can drop me off there," David said as he pointed to the building. He fumbled with his wallet to pull out the bills. "Here," he said, handed them over and began to open the door before the car had come to a full stop.

"Good luck in there." The driver was an older man, with a gray beard and wrinkles at the corners of his eyes that deepened as he smiled. "Whoever this Amanda is, I hope it works out for you."

David had not told the man why he was hurrying to town, but of course he had overheard his conversation with Naomi. "I never said it was about that..."

The man chuckled as he folded the bills and tucked them into his pants pocket. "You didn't have to. Now go tell her how you feel."

David beamed. "That's exactly what I intend to do." He scrambled out of the car, slammed the door behind him and hurried across the front porch of the Feed & Seed. The old, weathered boards creaked as he pounded over them. He tore open the door and rushed inside.

Amanda was there, right in front of him. She looked up from the row of feed bags beside her. "David?" She frowned and stepped closer. "Is everything okay?"

David realized that he must look ridiculous, barging in like that. He was out of breath and disheveled. She might even think that there was some kind of emergency. He really needed to calm down.

But he couldn't. The rest of his life was riding on this moment.

"*Ya.* Everything's fine." He rubbed his hands over the front of his black broadfall trousers. His palms were damp with sweat. "I, uh, I have to talk to you."

"You came here looking for me?"

"*Ya.*"

"But nothing's wrong? No one's hurt?"

David took off his hat and clutched it. He needed something to hold, something to do with his hands. "No one's hurt."

The furrow between her eyes deepened. "Then what's going on?"

She looked so beautiful standing there in her everyday work dress, black stockings and starched white *kapp*. A piece of hay stuck to her apron and there was a smudge of dirt on her sleeve. She must have been doing the farmwork when she'd had to run out to the store. She looked so perfect in her own element. She was where she belonged—and it was also where he belonged. They were the same. The thought warmed him like a hot, comforting drink on a cold day. He wanted someone to engage him. He wanted someone to strategize with, to work side by side with, someone who would challenge him. He did not want someone to cook his meals and clean his house. He wanted a partner and a friend. He wanted Amanda.

"Do you know how beautiful you look right now?" David asked.

"How... What?" Amanda's hands flew to her hair and she tucked a lose strand beneath her *kapp*. Then she smoothed her apron and brushed at the stain on her sleeve. "I don't—"

"Yes, you do."

"David, I don't understand."

"That you're beautiful?"

"*Vell*, that, yes. I'm a mess. I've been with the goats all day. But it's not just that. What's gotten into you? Why are you here, telling me this?"

Now was the time to backpedal and try to save himself from the humiliation that might be coming. But he would not. "You are not a mess. You are perfect. You are Amanda, looking exactly how Amanda should look. Do you know that your face lights up and your skin glows when you're doing farmwork? I've never seen a woman more beautiful than when you were covered in mud and soapy water trying to rescue my goats. Or when you're leading the herd from one pasture to another, striding across the farmland like you know exactly what you're doing—because you do."

"David, I—"

"I've got to finish, Amanda," David interrupted. "Because if I don't, I'll never get the courage to tell you how I really feel. I've been a coward, but I won't be one now."

She stared at him.

"When you suggested that we get married, I wanted it to be more than a business arrangement, but I was too afraid to tell you the truth. I'm in love with you, Amanda. I want to marry you, but I don't want a marriage of convenience. I want a real marriage. I want to be your partner and your best friend. I refused your suggestion to join our farms because I didn't want to trap you in a marriage that was one-sided. Say no if you don't love me, Amanda. I don't want you to be stuck with me." David took a step forward. "But if you love me, then marry me. Marry me because you love me and not for any other reason."

Amanda kept staring at him.

David's heart pounded inside his chest as he waited for an answer. The room was so silent that he could hear the pulse in his ears and the creak of the wind against the windowpanes.

"Say yes, Amanda!" a voice shouted from somewhere beside him. David jerked his attention to the right and saw the shopkeeper leaning casually against the counter with a wide grin on his face. David had not realized that Billy was listening. He could not help but chuckle. He had just announced his love to the entire store, for any bystander to hear.

Amanda laughed too, and so did Billy. But as Amanda laughed, her eyes were clear and bright. They stayed on David. She walked to him and looked up at him. "Yes."

"Yes, you'll marry me?"

"Yes."

"Does this mean you love me?"

"Of course it does."

David whooped, picked her up and swung her around. She threw back her head and laughed even louder than before. He had never seen her eyes shining like this. When he set her back onto the floor, she leaned in, stood on her tiptoes and reached for his cheek. He had to stoop down so that she could kiss him. Then she whispered in his ear, "But I do have a few things to say to you, this time without an audience."

David smiled. "Take a walk with me?"

"I'd like that." She tucked her arm into his.

"Congratulations, you two," Billy said. "Your parents would be happy for you, Amanda. You would have made them proud, you know."

Amanda stopped to look over at him. Her eyes misted over and she nodded. "Thanks, Billy. That means a lot."

He tipped his baseball cap and returned her nod.

David led them out of the store and onto Mainstreet. A handful of *Englisch* tourists strolled along the sidewalk sipping coffee from to-go cups and carrying shopping bags. Amanda patted Clyde's neck as they passed him. "We'll be back soon," she said. The horse whinnied and stamped a hoof.

David was nervous to hear what she wanted to say. He wished they could just walk off into the sunset together, right then and there. But if she needed to communicate, then he wanted to give her the chance. That was the only way to start a good marriage. "So, what do you need to talk about?" he asked as they wandered toward the row of mom-and-pop storefronts.

Amanda glanced around, as if she wanted to be sure that there was no one to overhear. "I have a confession to make. And I've been afraid to tell you."

David braced himself. After all he'd been through to get this far, he refused to give up now. No matter what Amanda had to say.

Amanda had to make things clear to David. It was the only way. Neither of them would be happy if he had expectations that she could not, or would not, fulfill. But even so, it was hard to force herself to say the words. Everything felt so perfect and she could not bear to shatter the moment. Never in her life had she expected such a proposal. Her heart was still pounding in her chest from the joy and excitement. David had gone after her, sought her out and declared his love. It was more than she had ever hoped for.

But she had to be certain that it was what she thought it was. She had to be sure that he would not regret it years down the road, when he realized that she would never be the homemaker that her other Amish suitors had wanted. Some men married believing that they could mold their wives into what they wanted. David did not seem like that sort of man. In fact, Amanda was sure that he was not. But she had to ask, for both their sakes.

The traffic light changed, and he took her hand and held it as they crossed the intersection. It seemed so right to have his hand in hers. She was vaguely aware of cars idling nearby, but nothing felt real but him.

David glanced down at her, then moved his attention back to the sidewalk in front of them. A shop door opened behind them and a bell chimed. Someone laughed in the distance. David cleared his throat. "It's okay. You can tell me." His hand tightened around hers. "Whatever it is, we can get through it together."

"I can't be the wife that you might want." There, she had said it, plain and simple.

David shook his head. "But what's the confession? What have you done?"

"It's what I won't do. I won't be a traditional Amish homemaker. I have to keep working with the goats. There're other people at Stoneybrook Farm who focus on the cooking and cleaning. Emma and Naomi prefer it to farmwork. And I help out, of course, but I prefer the fields and pastures. I like to do the outdoor jobs."

"I know."

"Right, but when we get married…"

"I don't think you understand." David stopped walking and turned to face her. "I love you because of who you are, not because of what you might do for me. I love you because you love the outdoors and the farmwork. It's what makes you, you. And I want to work side by side with you. I never dreamed that I would find a *frau* who wanted to do that with me. It gets lonely working alone, you know."

"*Ya.*" Amanda could barely get the words out. Her head was spinning too fast. "I know. But what will people say? It isn't proper."

"There's nothing wrong with it. Let them say what they will, while we go on being happy."

Amanda felt a warm wave of warmth spreading though her. If she just let go and trusted him, then she could fall into this dream and never have to lose it. This marriage, this man, was everything she had ever wanted, but never dared to hope for. But there was still more to say. "I guess I have more to confess."

David squeezed her hand. "Whatever it is, it's okay." They fell into step beside one another again. Amanda noticed that he was walking slowly so that her short legs could keep up. Not all men were that considerate, or even thought to notice.

"I've been rejected by every suitor because I refuse to be the traditional *frau* they expect me to be. It's why I pushed you away. I figured you would feel the same way as the others."

David frowned. "But I already knew that about you from your letters. And I admired you for it."

"*Vell*, *ya*, it seemed that way in your letters. I fell in love with you back then, before we had even met, even though I had no idea what you looked like. One of the reasons was because you understood me and supported me."

David glanced over at her with a sly grin. "So you fell in love with me back then, huh?"

Amanda blushed but met his eyes. "*Ya.*" She loved how warm and expressive those eyes were. She felt safe when she looked into them, her hand in his as they strolled side by side.

David's smile turned wistful as he looked at her. She could sense that his playful mood had shifted, and she wondered what he was thinking. He dropped his gaze and nodded toward the town square. "Let's sit down. It's my turn to make a confession now." He led her past a row of flower beds, and they settled onto a park bench beside a fountain. David took a deep breath. "I guess it's pretty obvious."

"What is?"

"That I pushed you away because I was insecure."

"But you were never insecure in your letters. You were more than willing to ask for advice."

David rubbed the back of his neck. "*Ya*, but then I met you and…" He dropped his hand and picked at a loose thread on his black trousers. "You were so perfect. How could I not be intimidated?"

"You were intimidated by me?"

David sighed. "*Ya*. And a little jealous. Okay, a lot jealous. Especially before I knew it was you, M.M."

"So, that's the way you were feeling at the livestock auction?"

"*Ya*. And then at the feedstore when we ran into each other."

Amanda sat for a moment without speaking, thinking over what he had said.

David leaned an elbow on the arm of the bench. "That's why I kept giving you a hard time."

Amanda put a hand on his arm. "And I may have gloated. Just a little."

David smiled softly and put his hand over hers. "I was afraid you'd see me for the failure that I am."

Amanda straightened up. "Failure? How could I ever see you as a failure?"

David's brow creased. "How could you not? I've lost my farm. I couldn't make a go of it." He squeezed his eyes shut. "I just wasn't *gut* enough."

"You're seeing it all wrong."

David opened his eyes, but he didn't look at her. He studied the water as it splashed from the fountain and into the basin. Sunlight shone through the droplets and made moving ripples underneath the surface.

"You did everything you could," Amanda continued. "But what matters more to me is that you value the right things. You love the people around you for who they are, not for what they can do for you."

A small smile appeared on David's face, then spread into a wider one.

Amanda squeezed his arm. "And you know me well enough to know that I don't tell people things just because they want to hear it."

David chuckled. "That's true." He glanced at her, then back at the fountain. "So, you don't mind that I've failed at farming."

"I just told you that you haven't failed."

"*Vell*, I've lost my farm, however you want to put it."

"You haven't lost a farm, David. You've gained one."

David's attention swung back to her. His eyes were full of unspoken longing.

"You're marrying into the biggest goat farm in the county. You'll own and operate it along with the rest of us. It'll belong to you too."

"But you like your independence."

"*Ach*, David. I don't think you understand. I want to partner with you. As long as we are equals, then there's nothing I want more than to work with you every day."

"So you won't feel like I'm taking over."

"Do you plan on pushing me out and taking over?"

"*Nee*, of course not."

"Then why would I feel that way?"

"Because you want to run things on your own. It seems really important to you. I want to honor that."

"I don't need to prove that I can do things on my own anymore. I know that you see me now."

"I do, Amanda. I really do."

She felt a wave of warmth spread through her, as bright and comforting as sunshine on a summer's day. "You don't have anything to prove anymore, either. I love you just the way you are. This—" she tapped his chest, over his heart "—is more important than any accomplishment. What is the point of a man earning a *gut* income, if he doesn't treat the people around him with love and respect?"

"So, you're not embarrassed by me? You're a lot more successful than I am, you know."

Amanda laughed out loud. "You're judging success the way the world does."

David smiled. "I guess I am." He turned his gaze to hers. "But I won't anymore."

Amanda swallowed hard. She could feel the connection pulsing between them. "When can you and your family move in?"

"All of us?"

"Of course." Her eyes moved to his lips. She had never been kissed before. This would be the perfect moment.

"As soon as possible," David murmured.

Amanda's heart beat harder. The air shimmered between them, full of expectation. David leaned closer. The moment turned to slow-motion as her pulse pounded in her throat. And then his lips reached hers and he kissed her.

It was the perfect kiss, for a perfect moment. Amanda knew that she was loved and valued. And nothing could ever take that truth away from her.

They would spend the rest of their lives together, living out a beautiful, shared dream. Because, apparently, dreams and fairy tales really could come true, especially when the prince was not afraid to be himself, and he loved a woman who knew exactly who she was.

Epilogue

Dear David,
I never thought I could feel this way. I don't have
to prove anything to anybody anymore. For the
first time in my life, I know that it's okay to be who
Gott made me to be. You helped me see that. Be-
cause you see me for exactly who I am—and you
love me for it.
      Thank you for being you.
Love Always,
Amanda

Sunshine poured over the south pasture, turning the grassy meadow to molten gold. David watched as Amanda called out commands to Chocolate and Chip and the dogs took off to round up the goats. The sun shone against her white apron and *kapp* as she stood above him on the hill, silhouetted against a bright blue sky. A warm breeze swept up from the valley, carrying the scent of earth and wildflowers. In the distance, bells chimed as the goats picked their way toward a new grazing field. Amanda turned toward David, threw a hand up in a wave and smiled. David never wanted to forget this moment. Amanda looked so alive, so happy and free. And he was happier and more in love than he'd ever thought possible.

The Amish did not take photos, so he stood for a moment, taking in the scene so he would always remember how blessed he was.

"We should head back to the house," Amanda said, loudly enough for her voice to carry to him across the field. "It's probably close to suppertime."

"*Ya.*" David watched as the goat herd drew near. He opened the gate beside him and waited as they filed in, bleating and twitching their tails. Chip barked at a stray nanny, then circled the herd to keep them moving. Chocolate took off in the opposite direction to bring back a wandering kid.

Amanda trotted partway down the hill until she reached David. He pulled her close and planted a kiss on top of her head. "You look beautiful."

Amanda laughed. "I'm covered in mud and my hair's falling down." She pushed a stray strand of hair back under her *kapp.*

"Happiness brings out your natural beauty, I guess."

Amanda rolled her eyes, but she was smiling. "I never thought you'd be so mushy."

"Oh, I can get way mushier than that." He winked at her and she laughed again.

"Sometimes I don't know what to do with you," Amanda said.

"Did you like it better when we were fighting, back when we first met in person?"

Amanda laughed and slipped her arm in his. He thought that she was going to tease him back, but instead her expression shifted into seriousness as her eyes swept over the farmland spread before them in a carpet of green and gold. "Are you happy too? On this farm, I mean." Her eyes flicked to his. "I was afraid you might miss your own farm."

"We lost the farm I grew up on years ago—the one that had been home. The farm I had before we married was *gut*, but this place is a lot better." He swept his free arm in front of them. "Just look at it all. We've got acres and acres here, plenty of room for all of us. In fact, there's more room in the *dawdi haus* that John built for my parents and sister than in that farmhouse we were living in. It was a *gut* farm and I was thankful for it, but I prefer living here. We all do."

"*Ya*, it's a *gut* thing that John is a builder and there were plenty of folks to help him get the job done. Comes in handy around here." Amanda sighed and leaned closer to David. Her head rested against his bicep. "I'm so relieved to hear that you like living here. I wasn't sure it was the right thing to do when you suggested we sell your place, even though it was the only thing that made sense business-wise."

"I was attached to running my own farm and giving my family a home of our own. I've got that here." He breathed in deeply, inhaling the fresh country air. "This place is more than I could have hoped for. And I have a stake in it. That means something. It feels so *gut* to have a place of your own. That's what I really wanted." David remembered how he had longed for this when he was crouched over an assembly line in the windowless factory.

"Yes," Amanda murmured. "A place of our own."

Below them, farther down the long, sloping hillside, they could see the big, rambling farmhouse where he and Amanda shared a room. The new *dawdi haus* stood nearby, its coat of fresh white paint gleaming in the evening sun. A small figure raced through the backyard, the skirt of her dress snapping in the wind as she chased Belinda. Even though he could not make out her features from this distance, David could tell that it was Katie, running free through the farm, living the life he had always wanted for her.

Two figures emerged from the door of the *dawdi haus*, arm in arm. They were talking to one another, and the distant, faint sound of laughter carried up the hill on the breeze. Ever since they'd moved to Stoneybrook Farm, his father's back did not stoop quite so much, and the worry lines on his mother's forehead had softened.

"They look happy," Amanda said.

"They are." David smiled. "And I think your family is too. I thought it might be too crowded, but somehow it all works."

Amanda laughed. "Oh, there's always room for one more at Stoneybrook Farm, L.D."

David pulled her closer as they surveyed the land they loved, knowing that they would all have a home here together, forever.

* * * * *

Dear Reader,

Welcome back to Stoneybrook Farm! I hope you enjoyed the second book in the miniseries. As Amanda pointed out to David, there's always room for one more at Stoneybrook Farm, so be sure to return for the next novel, when Naomi will get her chance to find love. The third story from this big, rambunctious, warmhearted family will be available soon.

In the meantime, you can find me on Facebook @VirginiaWiseBooks and Instagram @virginiawisebooks. I'd love to connect with you there. For extra details that I don't share on social media, visit my website, virginiawisebooks.com, and sign up for my newsletter. Thank you for reading my books and staying in touch. It's always a joy to welcome you into my life, just as the Stoltzfus sisters welcome friends who become family.

Love Always,
Virginia Wise

Get up to 4 Free Books!

We'll send you 2 free books from each series you try PLUS a free Mystery Gift.

FREE
Value Over
$25

Both the **Love Inspired®** and **Love Inspired® Suspense** series feature compelling novels filled with inspirational romance, faith, forgiveness and hope.